The Witches of Isle Royale

The Witches of Isle Royale, Volume 1

M.A. Ryan

Published by M.A. Ryan, 2023.

To Cath, my greatest supporter.

And to Colin, for all the nights we read.

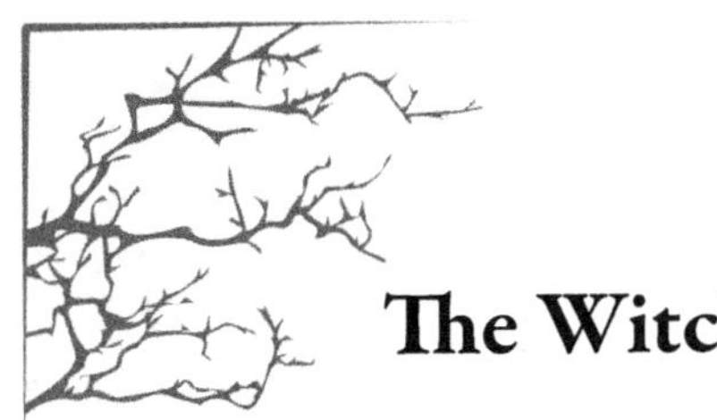

The Witches of Isle Royale

by M.A. Ryan

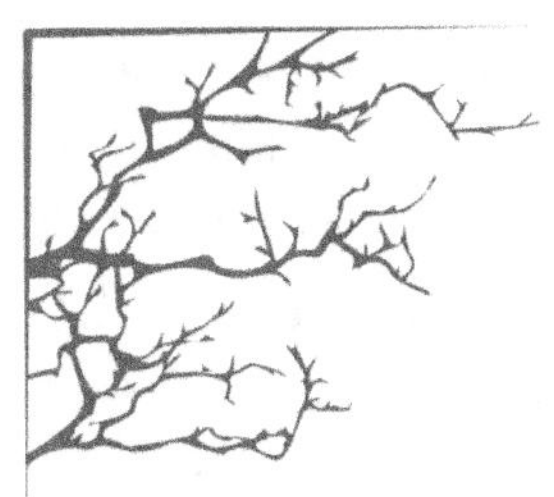

Prologue

Nothing was like it used to be. My father used to tell me what the country was like before the Collapse, and sometimes it doesn't seem all that different. The Northeast Regional Sovereignty isn't as big as America used to be, but it stretches from the Great Lakes to the Adirondacks, dips down into the Ohio Valley. Big enough, I guess, and it runs. More or less. Dad never did like the way Howard's temporary restoration government somehow became permanent – "God damn aristocracy" he used to say – but he went to work, raised a family, did what he was supposed to do and his ashes are scattered up in the old State Lands where he used to hunt and nobody goes any more.

Not like it used to be.

I suppose I could have run the blockades and got across the Mississippi to live in the Central Zone, but the CZ is a bigger shithole than the Sovereignty, least from what I can tell. It's too hot for my tastes down in the Confederacy, plus I'd have to get through the Wastelands below Wilkes-Barre and past the old capital. They say D.C. still glows at night from the anarchist backpack nukes. The whole Deep South never appealed to me much anyhow, and the Gold Coast...a played out pyrite mine. Dad said their overboard progressive tendencies got them what they deserved and he referred to it as "That chaotic clusterfuck on the other side of the Rockies."

So I went to school right here in the Metro area, did my hitch in the Reserves defending the border along the Wastes keeping the ragtag, the bandits and berserkers at bay, and stayed in the M after I mustered out. I worked, paid my taxes, even voted a few times casting my ballot against the aristocracy, kind of in memory of my father, but it didn't do any good. Things stayed the same, not like they used to be. When I got tired of working in the grocery store and took up private investigation I didn't bother getting a Sovereignty license, just worked under the table. Didn't bother paying taxes on my income, either. All the social benefits and financial security programs had been bled dry and recast as unaffordable Third Estate entitlements when I was a kid, so what for? I sometimes wonder if I'm as disillusioned as my dad became, or if he came to not care as much as I don't care now. Sometimes I wish I could ask him. If I could I'd also ask him what he ever heard about Isle Royale. I'd only heard to stay away from it and to turn in anyone from there that I might encounter. I don't think most people knew anything at all about the witches. I know I didn't until that night in Jack's Place.

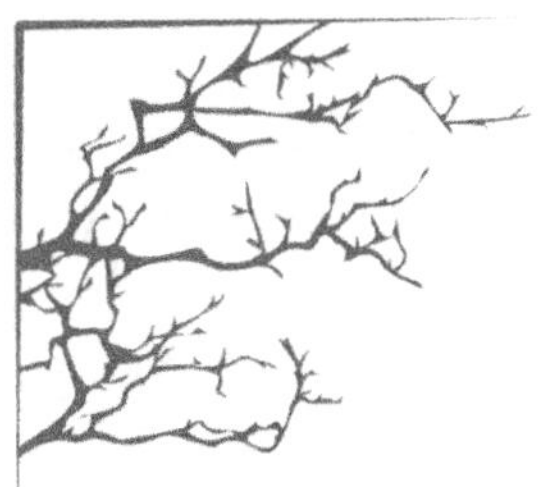

Chapter 1

She didn't look like a witch. No warts or gnarly knuckles, no ugly long nose. Nothing like that. She had a nice nose, ingenuous oval features and a cameo complexion with chestnut brown hair intricately braided in an attractive chignon.

Glass clinked beneath conversation and laughter, of numbers bets being placed in the thin haze of tobacco and stick smoke that gave Jack's Place a surreal look. The piquant smells alone were enough to get high on, but didn't trouble me sitting in a back booth as we were. The morality of it doesn't bother me, either. I do a lot of my business out of Jack's seeing as I don't have an office – don't have a license – and Jack sends clients my way now and again so I don't much care about drugging at the bar. Beer's my preference. Or sake when I can get it, but Jack doesn't stock that.

I sipped my beer and regarded soft brown eyes across the table. "You're looking for passage on the lakes."

"Can you help me?" she asked quietly, hands folded demurely on the table. "I want to go home." She was probably running, but though her simple loose black top and black pants hinted at fugitive status she was calm and collected, looking not at all like a frightened rabbit, someone on the run in this soul-corroding shithole that tramples people without a second thought. She didn't look as though she belonged here at all with dregs, drunks and bookies at the bar. I wondered if she thought I looked like a resident. Her gaze was steady, more curious than anything. "The man serving drinks said I should talk to you, the Japanese man."

"That'd be me. Kim Murayama. And you?"

With the beginnings of a small smile she replied, "My name is Mick."

Mick. I liked the name. And the way she said it. I wasn't sure it fit her, but it interested me. For some reason I couldn't immediately pinpoint, *she* interested me. "Mick what? Last name?"

She cocked her head and gave me a quizzical look. "Only Mick."

Incognito, then. Okay. "You running?" This perplexed her. "Are you UD?" I wasn't necessarily averse to helping her out even if she was. If the price was right.

"What is U-D?" She articulated it carefully, utterly unfamiliar with the acronym. That hoisted a red flag.

"Undocumented," I replied carefully. "Do you have a plate? For identification." Purchasing, riding the Tube. The bus. I wondered idly how she'd gotten to Jack's from wherever she came from. You can't live in the M without a plate. Well, you *can*, but it isn't much of a life. Not that life here is all frolic and merriment to begin with.

She said, "I am not from your great city."

I ran a finger up and down my beer glass drawing thin lines in the condensation while I considered this. Maybe she was Canadian or maybe she just didn't know the difference between authoritarian guvy and a monarchy, but either way she was definitely fresh off the boat in the Northeast Sovereignty.

"Where are you from, then?" I raised my glass, watching her over the rim.

"Isle Royale." She said it right out as though no one might overhear.

"Shee-it." I almost choked on my beer. I didn't know a ton about Isle Royale but I knew it was prohibited and anyone off it is contraband. A "witch." Whether the obscure, little-known and seldom spoken of inhabitants were really dangerous, malicious crones with a bounty on their heads or if that was just more Ministry of Information saturation hype to encourage people to turn them in, the woman across from me appeared in all respects to be undocumented and I might be pinched as an accessory just being in her company. I glanced at Jack surreptitiously watching me.

"It is in Lake Superior," Mick went on, heedless. "Near Thunder Bay."

"I know where it is." If she'd told Jack that he could already have made a call. I had the sudden urge to vamoose and stood. "Come on."

"Where are we going?" She slid out of the booth, not nearly as skittish as she ought to be for her circumstances, more evidence that she didn't have a clue.

"For a walk. This isn't a good place for you." I threw some Bs on the table and we waded through the haze, Jack's hungry eyes following us all the way out the door. On the walk I checked for police. Nothing yet. I gestured in the direction of the Strip a half block on where we could hop the Tube.

Mick fell into step beside me. "Why must we leave?"

"Because you ain't got a plate."

"This is bad, yes?"

"UD is bad." I looked her up and down. "You really from Isle Royale?" She nodded ingenuously. "That's even worse." A thousand B worse. Even if the stories were bullshit, some myths can be very lucrative.

We crossed the street and headed toward the glare and noise of the Strip. I touched Mick's elbow, guiding her around a group of lounging streeters holding up the side of a dull red brick building smeared with graffiti that I recognized as Wall Flowers' tagging – a bleeding heart and purple foxglove growing by a river of blood. Greene Isaac's outfit. These bums in their post-apocalyptic burner jackets were somewhere between steampunk and diesel-delinquent. There was a pair of daffy welding glasses, what looked like a bionic armored gauntlet on another guy and gallons of ink showing on everybody everywhere not covered by all this imaginative fashion. Way too anachronistic, and unrealistic, to be with the Flowers.

Smoke drifted, a pungent mix of straight tobacco, marijuana, and a hint of some other psychedelic leaf currently popular with trendsetters and now filtering down to the lower lifeforms. Neon eyes tracked us, but none of them made a move. Mick stared with all the naivete of someone utterly unfamiliar with the process of devolution going great guns in the M.

"Who are those people?" she wanted to know. "They look strange."

"They *are* strange." One of them had a slime-green reptilian tail that made me think of an iguana. I hadn't seen that particular permutation before, but it didn't surprise me. Swallow the right DNA modifier, you can grow whatever you like. I've always wondered if the process can be reversed should something you don't anticipate grows somewhere you don't want it. A lot of bathtub brew from down below the Dead Line in the Kamaly isn't produced under real stringent quality control, so I suppose such a thing could happen. Me, I never changed, never swallowed any of the mods that are so popular with these trailblazing buffoons, so I don't know for sure. Or much care. The Collapse has had a cataclysmic effect on all of us, but changing isn't my idea of coping. "They're goofballs," I told Mick, "Stay away from them. All they'll do is cause you trouble."

"There is much trouble in your world, yes?"

My world. As though I had any influence in it. I almost laughed. "If you don't like it, you didn't have to come here."

"I did not choose to," she assured me. "They brought me here. Thompson and the men on the ship."

Kidnap, then. Off Isle Royale? What the hell for? Far as I knew whatever folks were on the island were quarantined, and you hardly need to go to the ends of the Great Lakes to impress prostitutes. I suppose the Syndicate could afford to do that, but it doesn't have a GDP equal to or greater than the Sovereignty's because it wastes money. There's plenty of hooker material just on the God damn Strip. Mick came to an abrupt halt.

"Is that what you think I am?" she demanded.

Jesus. I came up short myself. *Did* she know what I was thinking? Maybe the stories were more than just fairy tales. Traffic sounds and the drifting, heavy thump of clashing music leaking out of watering holes up and down the Strip receded; her eyes grew wider, the kind of yawning deep you fall into and never get out of. It wasn't easy, but I kept my expression flat, just staring at her. After several long heartbeats during which I didn't fall in, I shook myself and resumed walking. "We need to get you out of the M. This Thompson'll be after you. Or the police will." Or both.

She scooted to catch up. "You are not afraid of me."

"Should I be?" I asked absently, scanning again for any sign of interest in us that we didn't need. She didn't answer me. Maybe she knew what I was thinking and maybe she didn't. What difference? No one wanted to be caught with a contraband loose off her quarantined island. No secret that.

We turned a corner into the full, glorious blaze of the Strip, a whirlwind of bleeding neon and flashing lights from the front of gin mills, porn shops, tattoo parlors and bawdy houses, the street picketed by working girls, pimps and dealers. Horns blared as aggressive-line muscle cars cruised, old Chevy's with big-block 450s still rolling, a yellow 340 Duster with black striping and 325 horses under the hood that would have been a classic *before* the Collapse. Always liked those. Never had one, but always liked them. A garishly painted low-rider eased along, bouncing on its hydraulics, probably one of Greene Isaac's fleet. Mick took all this in with a wide-eyed wonder. A Tube stop beckoned a block up. Unthinking, I took her hand and pulled her after me. "Where are we going?" she asked again, more curious than desperate.

"The docks. To see about getting you a lift home."

Half way to the Tube stop the streeters reappeared, led by the Tail. They came up fast from behind and to the side. "Hey, you Bakery Man!" The Tail jumped in front of us, glitzy red eyes shining. His growth twitched. I bit my tongue and started to go around him, trying to avoid a spectacle in the street, but he sprang again. "Bakery Man, hey! Don't run, play." His companions, two young men and two young women, the latter decked out in ruffled Capris, leather cinchers and slave bracelets, circled us. They were just rowdies, but they were going to be a pain in the ass.

I stopped, showed them an affable smile and empty palms. "Excuse us. Please."

The Tail's lower lip protruded, freakishly festooned with silver and black horseshoe rings. "Bakery Man make sadness. Bakery Man make all things sad."

"I'm not from the bakery," I told him. "Please excuse us."

"No Bakery Man?" He leered at Mick. "Fib me big. Got fresh hot tart." He reached for Mick. She jerked back, scowling owlishly. The streeters guffawed.

I took a deep breath and tried one last time. "Excuse us."

Laughing louder, the Tail went for Mick again. She sprang back, surprisingly agile and balanced. I snatched the young man's hand, twisting it over and around in a compression wrist lock. He yelled and tried to pull free, but I applied more pressure giving him some real pain to think about. His knees half buckled, his expression a twisted grimace of surprise and shock. I pulled him close enough for intimate conversation. "Get out of the way, stupid. I'm not going to ask again."

"Ai! Bakery Man, okay, okay!" He sounded as though he meant to back down, but his free arm moved, hand arcing up toward my face. I automatically executed an outward middle block – *chudan-soto-uke* – stopping the punch. As soon as his arm struck mine it started back down and around in a classic knife fighting counter-strike. "Fucking Slant!" he snarled.

I shot a low block, catching the inside of his wrist and stopping that strike. The blow vibrated up my arm, but I ignored it and twisted the wrist I still held, snapping it before he could get a third try at cutting me. He screamed and the knife clattered on concrete. My knee slammed into his groin, doubling him. As he went down I delivered an elbow strike that knocked out a couple molars.

He groveled, one good hand clasped to his bloody mouth. I turned and threw myself back just in time to avoid another blade slicing for me.

"God damn it!" I arced a crescent kick. *Mikazuki-geri* smashed the attacker's knife hand in a chancy move that could have gotten my leg or Achilles tendon slashed if he was better or I missed, but he wasn't and I didn't. That blade spun off taking the metal gauntlet, which appeared nothing more than decoration, with it. I continued straight into *yoko-geri*. The side kick took him in the face and I felt his nose break. I leaped on him before he hit the ground, fingers closing around his throat. "You like knives?" I growled. "Huh? Do you?" The kid goggled. My fingertips pressured the cartilage rings of his windpipe and his tongue protruded, light glinting off a cheap imitation diamond stud through the tip.

I drew my free hand in close to my body, palm up, fingers rigid. "I'll rip your God damned heart out, you piece of shit."

Someone yelled. I dropped the piece of shit and spun into a middle stance. The third man was on the walkway, tangled in his burner jacket and neck beads, neon blue eyes crossed; the women stumbled away from Mick, hands raised as though to ward off evil. She faced them, her expression impassive, arms loose at her sides. Neon yellows and pinks wide, the women turned and ran. Mick stared after them for a moment, then looked at me and inquired solicitously, "Are you injured?"

I hate knives. I hate that one took everything from me once. I clenched my fists and glared at the streeter at my feet, imagining the lethal technique I'd threatened him with. I could do it. How I wanted to, but instead I swallowed and sucked in a breath. "I'm okay. You?"

"Uh, huh." Mick came over and put a hand on my arm, guileless brown eyes searching mine. She had to hear my heart hammering. "I think these people meant us harm."

"Without a doubt." I decided that she was indeed a cool cookie, but naive? My God. My head swiveled as traffic moved past. The night wound on, no one paying our show any particular attention. This horseshit happened on the Strip all the time. I took Mick's arm and we resumed our trip.

I WINCED SLIDING MY plate through the reader to board the Tube. It was a calculated risk that they weren't tracking me yet, depending on whether Jack had flipped me in and what he might have told the police. Piling on the misdemeanors I pulled Mick through the turnstile without paying for her. I was glad to note a security camera dangling from its wires, useless to that haphazardly maintained surveillance system. Half a dozen riders were scattered throughout the car wreathed in more color-clashing graffiti outside and in, hunched in on themselves, staring at their hands or the floor so as not to make eye contact with anybody. One slumped, appearing comatose. Mick surveyed this without a word, then sat by the dirty, streaked window and watched as we ground out of the station. The night gained speed as we headed north. At length she turned to me and murmured, "What is a slant?"

"Japanese." Normally I would have sidestepped her question. Pan-Nippon is embarrassingly rich with all the arrogance that goes along with that ascendance, looking down on the fallen, and it sometimes gets held against me as though the economic dump of the West Side is my fault. S'not worth hashing over, though. Things are what they are. I would have ignored the babe-in-the-woods query, but she caught me curiously unprepared. "It's not a compliment."

She regarded me in silence, the only sound the creak of the car and muffled clack of steel wheels. Eventually she said, "Are you rich, Mr. Murayama?"

"No," I replied slowly. "I'm not." I studied her sidelong, wondering again, but she just looked out the window and said no more.

The Tube deposited us two blocks from the waterfront and the rundown warehouse where Dave Hanson rented a corner office dockside. He leaned back and puffed on a briar pipe, cherry rum covering the worst of a mix of dead fish and brackish, greasy water. Wisps of fog seeped past the grimy window at his back while a half undressed pin-up girl on a curling, yellowed calendar two years out of date, Dave's only concession to interior decorating, gazed longingly out the window as though she'd rather be somewhere else.

"A witch, huh?" Dave hoisted his feet onto the barren desktop and leaned back, the worn chair groaning in protest. In the dim light of a single bulb his shoulders looked as broad as ever in a faded blue denim shirt, but I thought I saw a little more grey at his temples. "This is a new one even for you, Murayama." He studied Mick with a critical eye. "I heard about you. Never met anybody from the island, though. You really a witch?"

Mick edged behind me, her hand creeping into mine. I let her hang on and told Dave, "I want to take her back, bud."

"S'matter? You got something against a grand?"

I shrugged. "Don't need the money." I'd finished a job last week that would take care of the rent and beer for a couple months. The kid was dropping mods, changing down in the Kamaly and the old man wanted him back. It probably would have been better if he was left there, but Dad paid so I brought him back.

"Well, taking her to Isle Royale..." Dave shook his head slowly, scowling at his scarred desktop. "For one thing the island's posted. Nobody's supposed to go there. For another, nobody's paying. Unless you got money."

"This would be more like a favor," I admitted.

"A favor." He puffed and scrutinized Mick through the cloud rather like he might Pandora's Box. "I can take her west, Kim, but it won't be a favor. I can't afford that. I wish I could, but you know I can't. If we were going to Duluth or anything I'd hire you on for the run, but we ain't going up there right now. I'm sorry, man. I don't think I can help you with this one."

Mick tugged at my sleeve. "He will not take me home?"

"We're negotiating."

"We are not," Dave grunted. "Miss... what'd you say your name is?"

"Mick. My name is Mick."

"Mick the Witch. I wish I could help, but a trip to Lake Superior costs like hell."

She frowned. "I believe I detect an undertone of avarice."

I snickered. "Better hitch up your undertones, Dave. Your avarice is showing."

"It costs." He ticked off points on his fingers. "Fuel. Supplies. Payroll, tolls, grease. It adds up. And there's health insurance, income tax withholding, retirement. You know." He took in my disbelieving look and added, "Union dues. I got to have union dues. It's a closed shop. And besides..." He examined his pipe bowl. "She's a witch."

He didn't have to pay me anything. Never had before. And there was no union. It was all bullshit except that last. She almost certainly was a witch. "That really bother you?"

"Not unless I get boarded. Then they hang me, too, right alongside her off the yardarm. I'd prefer that didn't happen."

I didn't know if that was bullshit or not. I wasn't aware that contrabands were hung on the spot, although frankly I didn't know *what* they did with them. Never gave it much thought. Never needed to. "But if it was worth the risk, Dave?"

He rubbed his jaw thoughtfully. A thin stream of white curled. "If it was worth it."

Mick cleared her throat self-consciously. "Mr. Hanson. I cannot pay you anything now, but once we reach my home I can guarantee that you would be suitably compensated for your trouble. I am certain the amount would be most equitable."

Dave frowned, considering this. "I don't know. It'd be a lot of trouble. A *lot* of trouble, miss. And if I'm hung from my own yardarm..."

"Yes. Well." Mick cleared her throat again, tugged her top straight even though it didn't need straightening. "I doubt I could adequately compensate you if that happened."

"I sincerely doubt that you could."

Mick nibbled her lip. Island forests and cold waters hadn't prepared her for concrete, steel, and greed. Moisture glistened in her eyes.

A scuff from outside the office brought me around. The door slammed open and two roustabouts in coveralls stepped in with pistols leveled. Mick gasped and clutched my arm. I shifted, turning sideways to blade the intruders. Dave didn't move, but his expression went flat. Cold. I knew that look. I glanced at the window, gauging our chances when the shooting started. They didn't look good. Mick and I would never escape the bullets that way. We stood like statues for several long heartbeats, not a word spoken until a balding, heavy-set man in a cheap suit appeared filling the doorway. Breathing hard, he mopped perspiration from his brow with a limp blue handkerchief.

Thompson. Mick's voice sounded in my head. I gaped, shot a look at Dave, then the crowd. No one batted an eye. I was the only one hearing her. **A dealer in souls.**

So much for rumors. No wonder Dave didn't want to open the Box. Not that it mattered. Trouble was already loose.

"She's mine!" Thompson jabbed a finger at Mick hiding behind me.

"My apologies." Eternity was in those bottomless .45 maws; I spread my hands obsequiously and stepped aside. "Thought she was freelance. She's all yours."

Mick's disappointment washed over me like surf. I knew it was her, could feel it as Thompson stepped forward, reaching for her. I ignored the billowing black despair and grabbed his hand, twisting the palm up and swinging hard from underneath with my other arm to blast the extended elbow. Not designed to bend in that direction, the joint broke with an audible crack. The man cried out, but I spun him around for a shield, knowing Dave would be moving. His chair banged and one of the roustabouts fired, the report ricocheting sharply off the walls and ceiling. Brilliant orange muzzle blast exploded like the sun. Thompson spasmed and grunted wetly. Thunder roared twice more from behind me and one of Thompson's men lurched. He thrust his gun hand forward, managing to pull the trigger and crank off a round before collapsing against the wall. The other man clutched his chest and stared stupidly at the blood welling between his fingers. No matter how hard he clenched his fist the red stream flowed. He looked up, kind of questioning, then his eyes rolled back. His knees gave out and he went down, his unused pistol clattering faintly in the ringing echo of the shots. I let go of Thompson. He didn't make a sound as he slid to the floor. Dave stood behind his desk, breathing hard, a compact black .40 caliber automatic still held in a two-hand ready position. The desk draw hung open, his old chair upended. "God damn you, Murayama." He lowered the pistol. "I really, *really* don't need this. Why the hell can't you stay downtown and leave me be?"

"Jesus, I'm sorry, Dave. I didn't know this was going to happen."

"You were followed. You were fucking well followed."

"I wasn't followed," I protested, knowing damn well Jack had made a call. Not to the police or they'd have been here now putting twistcuffs on us all, but to somebody. Mick huddled in the corner gripping her right arm. Witch blood trickled between her fingers and down the back of her hand, red and sticky just like regular peoples'. I knelt beside her.

"What?" Dave came around the desk. "Aw, Christ. No wonder your business is going to hell."

"My business isn't going to hell!" This sort of thing – clients being plugged – advertised exactly that sort of a descent. I ground my teeth and gently pried Mick's fingers away from the wound. "For crying out loud, Dave, how about a little help?"

"Shit." He hopped over one body for a quick look outside, then stuffed the automatic behind his belt and slammed the door closed. He scrounged in the desk and came up with a first aid kit. "Get outa' the way, Murayama." I sat back and let him work. He was always better at that in the Reserves than I'd been and he was better now. He tore the bloody sleeve and squinted. "Looks through and through. Does it feel like the bone's broken, ma'am?"

She shook her head, grimacing. "I think no."

Dave grunted, satisfied with this diagnosis. He dug out antiseptic and gauze, and got at the job. Mick never uttered a sound, only watched him without expression. Finished, he sat back. "She better have this looked at by a doctor, man."

I hooked a thumb over my shoulder. "We're gonna' have to get rid of these guys."

"I know how to dump a body. I'll get O'Connor. I don't need any more help from you. Where's my God damn pipe?"

I said, "This isn't my fault, you know."

"Bullshit. This is all your fault. If you hadn't come up here in the first place none of this would have happened. I told you before. The old days are over. It ain't like it was. We ain't like *we* were." His nostrils flared, but he settled. "Get her over to Fredericks. Get her somewhere, but get her out of here. You understand me?"

"I understand, Dave."

From the desk he pulled out a handful of plates, selected three and thrust them at me. "Use these, for Christ's sake. At least they won't tag you going back downtown."

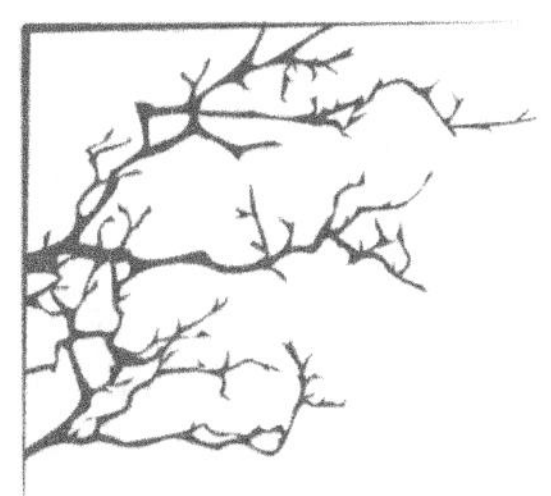

Chapter 2

Under ragged dark clouds hinting at nightmare, I helped Mick to the Tube. She leaned on me, heavier by the minute. Cheating the city out of a fare again, I swiped us both through as Herbert Waugette Upton, whoever he was and however he'd gotten in Dave's desk draw, and chose a barely occupied car. We took seats in the back; Mick sat with a stifled groan. One man glanced up disinterestedly, but no one else cared enough to even look. I leaned close to Mick. "How you doing?"

She smiled thinly, complexion pale. The Tube runs quiet, but still I nearly missed her reply. "I am frightened."

Understandable. I wanted to ask about head-to-head commentary, but the moment hardly seemed right. And she wasn't all that threatening and mysterious just now. She looked small and very alone. I gave her what I hoped was a reassuring smile. "Everything'll be all right."

"I am not at all certain I will not follow Thompson and those others to my fate. This place... your city, your friend Mr. Hanson. He seems... well, he seems sincere, but he is so gruff. So hard. He killed those men."

"Dave's a good man. He did what he had to do."

"He did not appear greatly troubled by the necessity."

I sighed at the pacifist sentiment. Dave and I have both done what we had to before, in the service and since. I'm not proud of some of those things and I don't suppose he is, either, but you do what you have to. Sometimes it's not pretty, but there's nothing to feel guilty about forever. I said, "They might have killed us all."

"That is what I mean. Your world seems so vicious. Even you..." She bit her lip. "I do not think you a beast, Mr. Murayama, but you fight so readily. So proficiently. The people of the street... It frightens me."

She didn't do so bad herself. I hadn't seen enough of that particular action to hazard a guess at what style she might be using, but my gut instinct said

Wing Chun kung-fu. Whatever it was she was well-practiced, disciplined and, I thought, a little spiritual about it. She didn't relish having had to dump that streeter on his ass.

"Did you intend to let Thompson have me?" Mick asked quietly. Her eyes searched mine for the answer she wanted to hear.

"No. I only wanted him to think that."

She shifted slightly with a barely detectable wince. "It worked quite well."

And three men were dead. They weren't the first, but it's never easy. Nor should it be. I watched the night rush by beyond the window, wondering if it could be some kind of conscience-stricken metaphor for what was in my heart, my soul repentant yet never atoned. After a while Mick laid her head on my shoulder. I thought about moving, then didn't.

We rode to the Chinese Wall without further conversation, debarking to make our way past the sprawling rail yard situated below street level. The block stone wall rising up to the Strip itself was supposedly built by Chinese immigrants way back when there was a country, back when anyone would have wanted to come in instead of dying to get out. Red, yellow and green signal lights shown from bracket masts and signal bridges below. Up above, the Strip still pulsed, its heartbeat always strongest after dark.

Doc Fredericks' doors stood open to the humid night. I ushered Mick up the steps and in.

It was a slow enough night at the clinic; Audrey was at the reception desk in what used to be the grand old house's foyer. She took us past the study, Doc's office now, and down the hall to Exam Room #1 which might once have been a bedroom before the place's grandeur faded like everything else in this world. It was only a minute before Doc entered, rubbing his hands together briskly, then wiping residual hand sanitizer on his already stained lab coat.

I filled him in as he made his examination.

"Isle Royale, you say?" Doc clucked his tongue, inspecting Mick's arm through a pair of Ben Franklin-style glasses perched precariously on the end of his nose. He glanced at me, then back to Mick. "You're a witch, then." It sounded very off-hand, not quite a question, gentle the way you'd use so as not to incite alarm or concern.

Mick glanced at me edgeways. "I only want to go home. Please."

"Mm, hmm..." Doc took a penlight and scrutinized the wound. "Got Master Murayama here to help you, eh?"

Her eyebrows rose. **Master?** drifted through my thoughts.

"It's an honorary title," I explained, doing my best to camouflage my renewed consternation.

"Don't let him kid you, my dear. He's earned it." Doc sat back and pushed his glasses up. "It doesn't appear mortal. The prognosis is good. Someone did a credible job of first aid. Kim?"

I shook my head, still frowning at Mick. "Dave."

"Ah. You boys ought to stay out of trouble." He leaned over a little, looking at *my* arm. "How's it doing?"

I touched the scar on my right forearm without much interest. It wasn't that long ago that he'd stitched it up after I got cut by a street punk in a little Greek coffee shop down on Monroe. I like to sit in a window booth and watch the freaks bop by. One of them came in and wanted me to get up and give him my wallet. I didn't want to get up and do that. A disagreement ensued. The cut was bad, but not as bad as my boy when it was all done. I told Doc it was fine.

"Good." He turned his attention back to Mick, carefully pulling down the lower lid of her right eye. "You must be tired, young lady. Up half the night having fun with Mr. Murayama." He reached for a syringe. "I'd like a blood sample if you don't mind. To screen for infection. We'll get you patched up and after that I'll give you a mild sedative. You can rest upstairs."

Mick smiled weakly, fatigue vying with apprehension. I fully expected another telegram to my head, but none arrived. I nodded in accord; we'd be safe here for the time being. Her shoulders relaxed. Doc cleaned and dressed the wound, got his blood sample and gave Mick the sedative. He offered to have an orderly help us get to the third floor where there were single and double rooms, and get us squared away, but I told him I could handle it. He led us farther down the hall to the creaking, almost antique elevator that made me consider taking the stairs from the foyer, but with Mick balanced on my hip I concluded that the trip to the third floor would be better accomplished via the lift. Doc advised the floor was unoccupied and once in the dimly lit corridor I pushed open the door of the first room we came to. I barely got Mick to the bed. She didn't protest when I removed the bloodstained black shirt; she wore nothing but the bandage underneath and I averted my gaze, though not with any whiplash speed. She was well proportioned in just the proportions I like things of that sort proportioned. If she *could* tell my thoughts I devoutly hoped she'd interpret them in the complimentary fashion I intended. I got no answer either way. Her head sank into the pillow with a sleepy growl. Her breathing slowed, turning soft and even. I covered her with the sheet and straightened, the restless clamor of traffic drifting up from the Strip, muted cries and shouts interspersed in the punk and headbanging heavy metal giving somebody down there an aneurysm. I listened to the maundering of the night and studied Mick's now peaceful features.

Witch. Could such a thing really exist? Reason argued no, but her voice in my head said otherwise. After a while I went to find Doc, taking the grand staircase curving down to the foyer, my palm sliding smoothly on the worn oak banister. A pot of coffee cooked over a Bunsen burner. Doc looked up from his microscope as I came in. "She's a witch all right, Murayama."

"That's what I hear." I used a beaker for a cup, holding the hot Pyrex gingerly. "She told me she's from Isle Royale. Everybody says that makes her a witch, but she hasn't said that."

"She doesn't deny it, though."

"I didn't cross-examine her." I sipped cautiously, still unwilling to completely surrender to my insistent suspicions. The coffee was old, almost too strong with that burned aftertaste. "Okay, she's a contraband. You want to turn her for the bounty?"

"No. I don't want the money. I don't want anything to do with her. I'd prefer she left."

This wasn't like the Doc Fredericks I knew when he was our battalion surgeon in the Reserves. "What the hell's gotten into you?"

He went to the window, contemplating something more than the night beyond the glass. "Your only interest is putting her on a boat for Lake Superior, right? I mean, there's no reason to dig up trouble, is there?"

"I don't know. What kind of trouble you got buried?"

He regarded me, rubbing his chin stubbled with a good two-day growth. "All right. Maybe you don't know. I find that hard to believe. You're a knowledgeable guy, but maybe you don't. Mark my words, though. The less said about this the better. Okay, then."

I listened attentively, my coffee growing cold as Doc explained that Mick's blood sample showed an elevated white count consistent with an Isle Royale witch. I didn't know the range of such counts, didn't bother peeking in the microscope – I'd have no idea what I was looking at – or ask how he knew, but that wasn't really necessary since they supposedly always have the same hair and eye color, a dead giveaway. Mick's brown hair and brown eyes... yeah, I'd noticed right off. Couldn't miss them. I speculated that she might be sick, given the elevated white count, but Doc said no. It was his contention that she'd never been sick a day in her life and probably never would be. She wasn't feeling too good tonight, but that was an injury, not an illness. She wouldn't catch a cold, the flu, Variant 91 or even Plague Y, and this immunity made her a commodity. "Her genes," Doc explained. "Cells. Ever heard of those? You have some yourself."

And on those cells are telomeres, little caps on the ends of the chromosomes. Our cells reproduce by dividing and after enough divisions the ends of those chromosomes start to get ragged. They lose their protective caps, the telomeres, except for those cells that produce telomerase. Telomerase rebuilds the telomeres and lets the cells keep going. Yeah, it keeps cancer cells going, too, but Doc winked conspiratorially and said, "If you know how to turn something on, you can calculate how to turn it off. You getting this at all now?" I thought I might be, albeit slowly. He parked a haunch on the corner of his desk. "You probably thought she was smuggled in for prostitution, didn't you?"

I kept my mouth shut, admitting nothing. Prostitution was a legitimate theory, but given what I was hearing, I judged her DNA the more likely explanation. Her telomerase. In human beings the production of that compound stops during fetal development with the notable but irrelevant exception of the reproductive cells where the amount is negligible. Unimaginably so. Research and any practical application requires far greater amounts of pure telomerase than can be obtained. As Doc recollected, research in the Southwest Confederation – Texas, then – cloned a gene that reactivated telomerase in human tissue samples. The whole idea was to make cells live longer than they normally do, but outside of a Petri dish it didn't work and therefore there wasn't any profit in it. It can't be synthesized, either, and surrogates don't produce it. Those were tried and there were some promising results, but in the end they didn't pan out. The Fountain of Youth wasn't in

Texas. And then we discovered the witches on Isle Royale, a virtually unlimited supply of telomerase.

How long have they been on the island? Doc didn't know. He recalled that they were mentioned in JAMA before the Collapse, in an article about injection vs. electrical current to fuse somatic donor cells with unfertilized eggs during reproductive cloning experiments. But that didn't say how the witches came to be there, only that they were. And if we could have their telomeres we could turn off cancer, eliminate disease, rejuvenate cells and stymie old age.

"We'd have immortality," he finished solemnly. "God blessed never die immortality."

It wasn't as far fetched as it sounded. You see 'mutes on the Strip all the time, moonshine DNA mods from down in the Kamaly. Same kind of thing except it didn't work. The Royales' telomeres do for them what we want them to do for us but don't, so after we'd wrung them out like laundry and could make no use of them, we cast them away. That's what we do – what the M does – with everyone and everything. The island's their reservation, a dumping ground for sinful indiscretion so we don't have to look our shitty transgressions in the eye. I lifted my gaze to the ceiling. "They aren't all locked away, though."

"No," Doc agreed. "They aren't."

The witches among us. I swirled rotten coffee in my beaker, studying it reflectively. "But if the stuff doesn't work..."

"Some people still search for El Dorado." Doc heaved himself up off the desk. "You best get her back to her island. They'll be coming for her. I'm telling you true."

There were three guys tonight who immortality wasn't going to help and that was the truth, too. I knew Doc didn't need this kind of trouble coming down the pike. I thanked him for his help and told him we'd be gone in the morning. Back upstairs, Mick was asleep, curled in a ball with the sheet pulled tight beneath her chin. A light blue blanket lay folded at the foot of the bed. I drew it carefully over her, then settled into the room's only chair to wait for some sleep of my own.

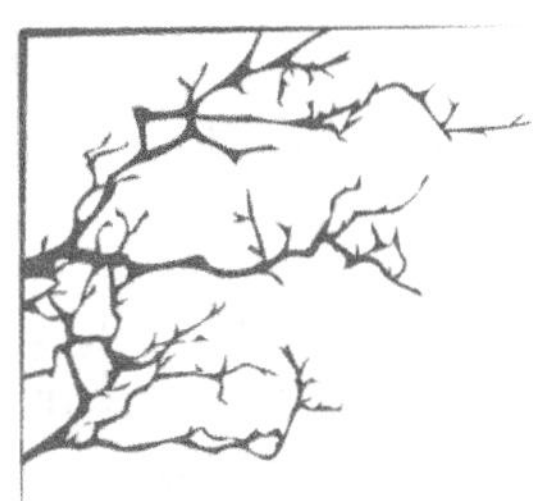

Chapter 3

I woke mid-morning, images of tombstones lingering at the edge of consciousness. I rubbed sleep from my eyes, erasing the last vestiges of the cemetery dream, and stood stiffly. Mick still slept.

Outside, tires splashed, people below hurried through the grey morning, hunched against a pelting rain. The bodega owner across the street had pulled his fruit boxes close under the faded blue and white awning while the pastor of the Grace Restoration Church of the True Faith or something like that urged the spiritually disenfranchised, the forsaken, and the sinners, of which there are plenty of each on the Strip, to seek shelter in his storefront house of salvation. Heavy, dark clouds promised only more of this weather, which wasn't necessarily a bad thing as it washed some of the city's grime down the sewers. From the corner of my eye I thought I glimpsed a pale, dark-haired young woman in a white dress disappear around the corner. It could have been Jo. I couldn't tell for sure, but the black hair... It could have been.

And if it *was*? Would I rush down and confront a ghost? I smiled grimly to myself.

"Who was she?"

I turned to find Mick cross-legged on the bed, the sheet pulled around her, eyes wide and penetrating, some vestige of night's shadows wrapping her. I had the unsettling impression that she wound the dusky umbra about herself. "Who was who?" I asked warily.

"Joanna."

My nails dug into my palms. "That's none of your business." I took a step toward her, suddenly half unglued without any idea why, one hand rising open-palmed for the shuto strike. Mick cringed and clutched the sheet to her chest, the strange duskiness dissipating. "You talked in my head and swiped my thoughts. Don't say you haven't, either. I never mentioned Joanna Rei to you." Jo's been dead for better than three years. I don't talk about her to anyone.

Mick's voice was almost a whimper. "Not even Mr. Hanson?"

"No, not even Mr. Hanson- God *damn*!" She was doing it! Right then.

"But you think of her often. You dream of her."

"Jesus H. Christ-" My fingers curled into a fist, arm quivering and still no idea what was torquing me enough to hit this woman or what it would fix if I did. I was scaring the hell out of her and out of myself as well. Slowly I fought down the unaccountable urge to do her violence and got control. My arm sank and I sighed. "Are you really this fatuous?" She didn't answer, only blinked at me. If she feared my wrath, she made no attempt to offer a defense or flee. Maybe because she was barely half dressed, but I judged modesty not the reason. I turned my back on her and stared out the window. "I don't think about Jo all the time. And even if I do, so what?"

"What harm would be done if you spoke of her now?"

I gave Mick a black look over my shoulder. "Why don't you just read my mind? That's what you're doing. Shit. Maybe Dave's right."

"Noo." She gave a tiny shake of her head, the denial a soft, breathy whisper leavened with a fragment of hope. A loose strand of her chestnut brown hair fell past one ear contributing to her artless mien. She started to speak, fell silent, then licked her lips and tried once more. "I know what you are thinking." She winced as though she'd just bitten her tongue. Or maybe her whole foot in her mouth. "That is, I am certain you are thinking that I know what you are thinking, and... ohh, I am not doing very well at this, am I?"

I softened a bit. She really didn't seem all that dangerous. "What exactly are you trying to do?"

"Explain myself. You think I know your thoughts because I am a witch and everyone knows about witches, do they not?"

"I'm not sure anyone knows the half of it." That got a tiny smile.

"They do not know so much as they think. Please believe me. Whatever stories you have heard are profoundly exaggerated."

"All of them?"

"Most of them." She gazed at me, expression now unreadable. Then, softly, "Are you afraid of me?"

I probably should have been, but all I said was, "I think we need to talk some more." A knock at the door interrupted. I opened it to find Doc's charge nurse Angel.

"I brought some clothes for your friend." She handed me a set of faded blue scrubs. "And Doc says you have a call. Downstairs."

I told Mick to get dressed and meet me, hustled after Angel without closing the door. In Doc's office, Dave was on the screen, aboard the *Lady*, the horizon banked up a distant grey-green behind him. I stepped in front of the screen. "What's up, pal?"

"My office is gone." His voice came through scratchy, but not hiding his choler. "The whole fucking warehouse is gone. They came looking for you and the witch and burned the place to the ground. There's two more stiffs."

"Immortality," Doc murmured. "God blessed never die."

Awful lot of people were getting dead instead of living forever. I wasn't sure I'd be on board with a program like that.

"You still got her?" Dave asked. "Yeah, okay, you do."

I almost started. Mick had materialized at my side as if by magic. She wore the blue scrubs, head slightly cocked, eyes wide.

The screen spoke. "She said I'd be adequately compensated if I took her home. Well, I need compensating now. Get her over to the pier in-" Dave checked his watch. "Half an hour. Be there."

"We'll make it. Who's dogging you?"

"God damn it, I don't know, but they were professional. Not like those slobs yesterday. Whoever you crossed is pissed at me now. How many times I asked you to leave me alone, huh? How many times I got to tell you things ain't like before. Jesus. You never listen. It pains me to admit that I may need your help now. Get your Oriental ass out here." The screen blanked.

I sent Mick to get her other clothes and thanked Doc again for his help.

He nodded gravely. "I warned you, Kim."

"I know." I should have warned Dave.

I PULLED FOSTER BALCH from my stash of plates and he got us on the Tube again without raising any alarms. I crossed my fingers that there wasn't enough left of Dave's office to tie him to any bodies lying around. Mick and I emerged from the Holden Street station a block above Ontario Beach and headed for the water down a buckled, crumbling sidewalk strewn with empty cans and broken bottles, past boarded up storefronts defaced with upside down crosses warning trespassers that this was The Unholy's turf. Unshaven loungers regarded us idly from the porch of one dilapidated old home, their gazes as blank as the broken windows staring at us like empty, lifeless eye sockets. Damp, leaden skies only added to the neighborhood's sagging depression and a subtle sense of foreboding.

"How's the arm?" I asked Mick absently.

"It is better," she murmured. She ran a hand up and down her bicep. "And yours?"

"My what?" I was more concerned with scanning the area.

"Your arm. The doctor asked after your condition."

I rolled my forearm, displaying the scar. It was still pretty red. "S'okay."

"What happened?"

"An accident," I muttered. I didn't care to talk about shitbirds with knives. She already considered me some kind of barbarian, or at least I thought she did, and part of me didn't want her to. We walked a ways in silence. I had the subdued but nevertheless distinct impression that she weighed my reply, or maybe its complete lack of depth. We reached the end of Lake Avenue where it hooks left and runs west as Beach Ave., lined with old, abandoned summer homes lonely or charred and gutted altogether, fit now only for vagrants and the dispossessed. I pointed in the opposite direction to a tattered, leaning chain link fence at the bottom of the hill. "There. The old amusement park."

"It does not look terribly amusing," Mick opined.

It didn't, no. Hasn't for years. I guess it used to be something Once Upon a Time – ice cream stands, merry-go-round, kids could swim in the lake – before the world changed. Now they were just as apt to step on an old needle or a busted patch, get mugged or get murdered with no one much caring about either. The police seldom came around, caring no more than anyone else. No, no place to bring the kids any more.

Across a broad, cracked parking lot serving only stripped and burned out hulks of automobiles, a group of streeters loitered, eyeing our progress. They were too far away to tell if they were wearing upside down crucifixes, but I judged them almost certainly with The Unholy. Another crew dressed in tight black leathers sauntered in from our right at a ninety degree angle. Their leader wore a sleeveless cowhide vest with long, dangling fringes, the kind of thoroughly out of place western motif that'd beat him to death in a high wind. The lot of them wriggled and shook like spastic idiots, doing Z or maybe the Power. We reached the end of the walk and I took Mick's hand, hurrying across the street.

"What did your friend Mr. Hanson mean when he said things are not the same as they were before?" she asked, breathing easily as we trotted.

"When did he say that?" I asked distractedly. Both groups were on the move, closing.

"In his office. And at the doctor's. He said you and he are not the same as before. What does he mean?"

"I don't really know." The lie came easily. Besides, now was not the time to discuss it. We were being flanked.

Mick recognized this, too. She hugged her parcel of clothes to her chest. "We should flee these people, I think."

She was a fast learner. We dashed up the walk and ducked through a break in the fence. Clumps of wild beach grass quickly gave way to dirty sand stretching down to lapping, dirtier brown water, carcasses of yellow perch scattered along the way. A squadron of gulls took off with a great, noisy flapping of wings and resentful squawking at having their meal interrupted. Ahead, small waves threw themselves against a cracked concrete pier stretching almost a half mile out into the lake. I pulled Mick along until we reached a tumbled-down concession stand not far from the pier. The round, one-story affair slumped mournfully, plywood tacked crookedly across its windows like band-aids on festering wounds. We crouched to catch our breath as I scanned the lake. No sign of the *Shady Lady*.

Mick tugged at my sleeve and pointed. A hundred feet off several carousel horses, lusterless paint peeling and cracked, lay tumbled about in an open-sided structure. Unseeing eyes peered at us from a long gone Yesterday. "Are they dead?" she panted.

I swallowed in a dry throat. "That was the carousel."

"A roundabout?"

Despite our immediate circumstances I couldn't help giving her a singular look. She had almost faultless diction and a distinctive vocabulary; her speech, other than the occasional colloquial "Uh, huh" was strongly vintage-flavored.

Rather than incongruous I found that idiosyncrasy curiously compelling. Like I found Mick curiously compelling. All I said, though, was, "Yeah. A roundabout."

She pointed again. Half a dozen streeters crawled through the same break we had used and jogged in our direction. They carried sticks, boards, couple of steel pipes. Mick abandoned her package and clasped my hands. "It is me they want, Kim Murayama."

"Well, they can't have you." At least not without a fight. I pulled her up, shoved her old clothes back into her arms and pushed her toward the pier. "Go. All the way out to the end. Dave'll be there." I devoutly hoped.

She hesitated for a moment, then ran. The streeters broke into a charge, yelling and waving their makeshift weapons. I sprinted toward them. An instant before we collided I leaped, tearing through their ranks with a scissors kick. Each foot struck home on either side, both in the head, knocking two of them cold.

I hit the ground and somersaulted forward, coming up in a middle stance behind the others. Two more put on the brakes, turned and rushed me. I used an outside crescent kick that got one in the temple, rattling his glowing orange eyeballs like marbles. I dropped low, continuing to spin, the *harai* technique sweeping the other off his feet. He landed with a grunt and before he could recover I was up. A snap kick to the head ended his participation in the festivities. The last two had gone after Mick.

"Son of a bitch." Their leading man with the Circle Bar D vest swayed erect, still conscious. He faced me, hefting his board. Now I could see Jesus of Nazareth dangling upside down around his neck. I'd have preferred not to mix it up with the Unholy – they carry grudges a long way – but they'd called how it was going to go. Over his shoulder I saw one of Mick's assailants already prone, not moving. The other swung a pipe. Mick slipped smoothly to one side, parried it, then struck with both hands, parallel knife-edges flashing into her assailant's throat. Positioning and style triumphed magnificently over brute strength. I heard him gag as he fell.

My opponent swore again under his breath, less certain than ever. "God damned Slants. Both of ya'. Nobody said nothing 'bout this." He made it sound twice as unsavory as just one of us and very unethical of their employer to overlook that aspect.

I grinned amiably and showed him empty palms. He wavered a moment longer, head moving back and forth in short, sharp little jerks, then threw down the board and stampeded for the fence, fringes flapping in the breeze. The next group was stepping through. They balked as the remnants of the first wave retreated.

I hopped over to where Mick stood looking down at the two she'd laid out like floral pieces, a trace of reticence on her oval features. "You okay, lady?"

She gave me a piercing look. For a fraction of a second I saw furious, unearthly light burning behind her eyes, a churning mix of malevolent passions fueled by anger and desperation. Almost instantly it vanished as though purposely snuffed out. "I am not injured."

Our pursuit still vacillated and we took advantage, collecting her clothes and running along the cracked, crumbling pier, dodging large gaps exposing rusted re-bar. Two hundred yards out a vessel heeled over, coming on hard. I recognized her lines through the haze as Dave's 85-foot crew boat. As we reached the end of the pier, scattering more gulls, he brought the *Lady* in tight, twin diesels reversing and churning filthy lake water to brown, foamy froth. His deckhand O'Connor, a genial, barrel-chested Irishman, was at the port rail to greet us, an old but eminently serviceable M2 carbine braced on his left hip. "Step lively, lass." He reached for Mick with his free hand. "We'll not be dropping anchor, that's sure."

I took a last look at the beach. The streeters could see the gun, too, and the 30-round magazine. Enthusiasm lost, they skulked away.

"Come on, God damn it!" Dave called from the flying bridge. "Murayama! Let's go!"

Still I delayed. I saw no one, but I felt them. They were there. Not streeters, either. Someone else. Someone not afraid of O'Connor's carbine. Finally, I turned and jumped aboard. My feet barely hit the deck when Dave gunned the engines and the *Lady* swung powerfully to starboard, stern settling deep as we headed for open water. I led Mick and we clambered up to the bridge where Dave had this overwhelming need to be pissed off at me.

"*You* came into my office with *her*." His first and last words were punctuated by an accusatory stab of the Inescapable Finger of Indictment at me, then Mick. "Then three guys came in after her. Then they got dead. Then more people came and my God damned office burned to the ground!" Struggling to maintain the little composure left him, Dave added thinly, "It's my considered opinion, Murayama, that these events are all related."

"You make it sound as though they're all my fault, too."

"I feel quite strongly that they are. And to make amends you can ride shotgun while we take your friend, here, back to the island where you can insure, just like you were my agent, that I get paid handsomely for all my trouble." He glanced at Mick. "Nothing personal, ma'am, but I did outline in my itemized estimate how much trouble it would be. Trouble is very expensive If you don't believe me, ask Mr. Murayama to explain it to you."

I made a face. "You ain't got no itemized estimate."

"Oh, yes, I do. Or rather, I did before people broke into my office and everything burned because *you* were there. Am I getting through to you, spud?"

"Loud and clear." I stood aside as he brushed past and dropped down the ladder.

"Don't be taking him too awful serious," O'Connor said with a chuckle. "He'll get over it." He gave only casual attention to tilling the *Lady*, perpetual grin in place. "Ye remember where the staterooms are. It's going to be a middling long trip at best."

I conducted Mick below to one of the cramped berths, hardly a stateroom but having an ocean view through its single porthole. I showed her where to stow her blood-stained black outfit under the narrow bed fixed to the bulkhead. She took in the spartan quarters without comment, her expression impassive, then followed me back on deck amidships along the starboard rail. The skyline of the M receded, the lake surface slipping past, cold and dark, carrying us toward ominous black clouds rising in the west. The breeze of our passage plucked at Mick's hair. I studied her, wondering if immortality was really possible. It'd be a far cry from the results of moonshine mods distilled through some hillbilly flute down in the Kamaly. And could telomerase really account for an underground trade in souls? Cigarette boats packed with shanghaied unfortunates slipping into isolated coves in the dead of night. Blacked out trucks and unmarked vans waiting to haul away helpless human cargo to clandestine labs behind a facade of respectability somewhere in the M. Probably on the East Side where all the respectability is.

Pretty fanciful, though. Hell, even if it did work, who wants to live forever? Who could afford it? You ask me, the price would be so steep as to preclude regular folks from taking the cure. Still, prices reflect what the traffic will bear and traffic in the M is always heavy. Rush hour never stops. Doc thought the profit margin too low before the Collapse, but he wasn't a financial wiz. Maybe there was money to be made in life everlasting. I leaned on the rail and regarded Mick with renewed curiosity.

"No." She stared out across the lake, more interested in something only she could see. "I am not immortal, Mr. Murayama."

"Really." No talking in my sleep this time. It was out and out larceny, but I held myself in check. Mick turned slowly, eyes wide and penetrating. The air grew suddenly sharp, almost frigid. From the thunderstorm coming on, a cold front. In the deep, dark recesses of my subconscious where we keep the things we learned to be afraid of, I knew different.

"I am *not*!" she whispered fiercely. Almost instantly she relaxed and the arctic chill vanished. Mick scowled for a moment, then drew in on herself. "You have no idea how mistaken you are. You are more immortal than I. I shall not live half so long as you." She lowered her gaze. "Please. I only want to go home."

"You're going home. I promise. But by God we really, really have to talk."

She nodded, pushing back the intransigent strand of hair as the first large, fat raindrops began to fall. We headed below, no more than entering Mick's cabin than the squall broke. Sudden hard rain sheeted the porthole and pounded the lake surface, the storm rumbling and growling angrily around the *Lady*. Ignoring the tempest I planted my hands on my hips. "All right. Let's talk."

"Fine." The word came out brittle, followed by nothing more.

I cleared my throat. "I think the stories I've heard about you, about Royales, might be true, Mick."

"I told you. Those stories are greatly exaggerated."

"It was awfully cold out there a minute ago."

"The rain was coming," she muttered, her tone faintly suggesting that I was little more than a poor rustic huddled in the dark blaming some hapless old woman because my cow wouldn't give milk and the crops had wilted.

I changed the axis of my interrogation. "What did you mean when you said I'm more immortal than you?"

"Nothing."

"Bullshit."

"I beg your pardon?" Her expression shifted to one of challenge.

"I said that's bullshit. First you say you're not immortal, then you tell me I'm more immortal than you. Plus you've been talking in my head. And that *ain't* bullshit."

"Speaking without speaking." She frowned. "It is nothing evil, I assure you."

Her assurance wasn't particularly convincing. "You've been reading my mind, too. Don't tell me you haven't."

For several seconds she stared at me. Then, just as she was about to speak, a clap of thunder split the sky. Mick went stiff as a board, eyes squeezed shut, fists balled. She shook her head violently as another peal ripped the air. She shuddered and grabbed my shirt.

"Mr. Murayama-" The rest of her words were muffled against my chest as she clung to me in tears. I tried to hold her without being intimate, but that doesn't work very well. I gave in and drew her close. Rain drove relentlessly against the porthole's fogged glass, my conscience clamoring to be let in. A flash lit the cabin an intense, hot blue-white, then gone leaving it darker than before. Mick burrowed closer and sobbed. "It is the Darkness. It lives in the clouds. It burns the sky with swords of fire from beyond the thunder." Another tympanic crash detonated like to split the *Lady* from stem to stern. Mick squealed and buried her face in the hollow of my shoulder. "I swear I did not choose this! It is not my design!"

Still without answers I held her as the storm bellowed. Our faces were close together and somehow our lips touched. I tasted the salt in her tears. Her fingertips brushed my cheek and she whispered a broken apology over and over. I should have stopped then, but it felt good to have a woman in my arms after all this time, to feel her warmth and know she wanted to be there. Mick's breasts pressed softly against my chest through the thin scrub top and it felt good. Then we kissed, almost by accident except that can't really be an accident.

Neither can what almost happened next.

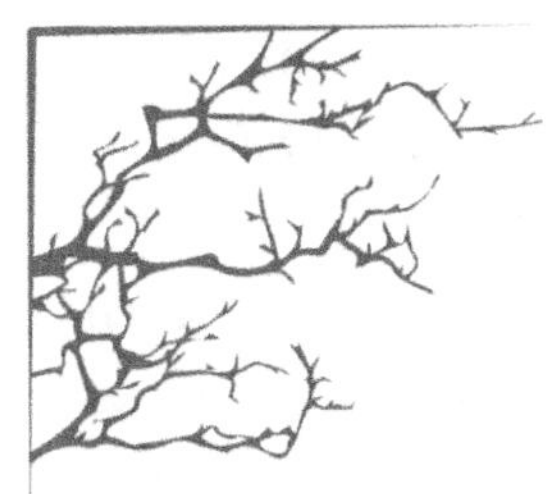

Chapter 4

I suppose Mick wanted to make love. I know I did, but my demons did a commendable job. Guilt and self-denial triumphed again. As the storm drifted away behind us with an occasional taunting echo of distant thunder, Mick sat at the head of the bunk, wedged into the corner hugging her knees to her chest. She struggled heroically not to cry, failing in the attempt. "You must think me most promiscuous."

"No..." I shook my head miserably and sank down on the other end of the bunk. "Look, it's not you."

"Then what is it?" she begged.

Because I nearly betrayed Joanna. I almost shouted, but bit it back. Mick intuited more than enough without hearing that. I remembered how she looked at Doc's, in the middle of the bed with shadows wound about her. Her eyes. Joanna was dead because I wasn't there when she needed me and those brown witch-eyes bored through every rationalization, interpretation, and homemade justification I ever constructed to conceal the fact.

"It was not your fault," Mick snuffled.

"Jesus Christ." I held my head. Could I block her out that way? I didn't think so. I know it wasn't my fault. I wasn't holding the knife. I know that. And I couldn't have predicted what happened. No one could. Sensei Shiyro's told me that, Dave's told me- Christ, I've told myself that more times than I can remember.

Mick wiped at her cheek with the back of her hand. "I thought you did not speak of the matter to Mr. Hanson."

She never stopped. No wonder they were quarantined. "I lied. I didn't want to talk about it."

"Will you speak of it now?"

"Why don't you just read my mind?" I growled.

"It is not evil!" she said tearfully. "I do not steal your thoughts!" Mick swallowed thickly, trying to compose herself. "It is not the way you believe, your thoughts to mine. I do not steal from you. It is more like the sun."

The sun. Master Shiyro would come up with something esoteric like that, some bizarre, hard to grasp Eastern philosophy. I arched an eyebrow, curiosity slowly replacing exasperation.

"The sun is warm," she ventured. "It touches me. I may seek the shade of a tree, but the air is warmed and I still feel it all around me. Like the air warmed by the sun, your thoughts remain. Different, but they remain. I listen to your words. I watch you. Do you smile? Are you sad. These things say much. Your eyes speak as well. You have black eyes. Like a Windigo."

"Like a what?"

"A Windigo. From the far end of the island where the winds blow." It told me nothing.

I shifted, drawing one leg up onto the bunk, studying her. Mick's eyes glistened in the half light, dark pools daring me to enter another world with other truths. I could have fallen in then – I started to let go this time – but the intercom saved me.

"The big canal's coming up," Dave's voice crackled. "Roll out of the rack."

Mick said nothing, her expression unreadable. I stared at her for several more seconds, then stood to answer the call.

THE SUN SANK THROUGH an ashen haze, a dull orange ball slipping down to where the water met the sky. I stood with Mick at the port railing as the Niagara River slid slowly past just the other side of the invisible international boundary. Half an hour and we'd enter the Welland Canal.

"Soldiers." She pointed to shore where moss-covered stone walls sloped up from the waterline; artillery muzzles sprouted behind the battlements of Fort Niagara. Even now, after the Collapse, NE Sovereignty troops garrisoned the fort, ready to repel a Canadian invasion. If it happened it wouldn't last long and we'd be speaking Québécois, but Canada's not going to invade. The Sovereignty's just paranoid. There's nothing left that anybody'd want. Mick regarded me sidelong as though debating whether or not to pursue the subject. At length she murmured, "You served."

It was my turn to debate with myself. Strange way to carry on a conversation, but I decided What the hell? So far all she'd done was make me feel uncomfortable, the way hidden truth can make you uncomfortable. "I was Fourth Infantry Reserve Battalion. Down below Elmira. The Wastelands."

Mick nodded, half to herself, then straightened, tucking a strand of the perpetually escaping hair behind her ear. "Are you sorry we did not make love this evening?"

"No." Caught flat-footed by her shift of gears, my face warmed. "What I mean is, yes. I am. I'm not and I am." I could have kicked myself. That's one of the stupidest half-ass exculpatory phrases you can come up with. I sighed. "Yes, I *am* sorry. It's not you, either, okay?"

"I am sorry, too. Perhaps another time...?" She inched closer, almost touching me.

"Perhaps."

"I should like that," she whispered.

I watched the shoreline for a while, but more watching Mick from the corner of my eye. I regretted the earlier insult with my speculation that she'd been abducted for prostitution. She was as far from a streetwalker as a woman could get. On the other hand, if she was forced into the business she'd have been high class commanding top dollar, the sort of companion you booked as an escort, not waved over on the Strip at 10 or 15B for a five minute job.

For just a moment I envisioned Mick in a dress or gown worth several hundred B instead of faded blue scrubs that had been washed a hundred times. Her best color would be black, as when I first saw her, but a dress. One with long sleeves and cut low, though not so daring as to be immodest, narrow gold piping at the neckline, wrists, and hem. It would reach just below her knees and showcase black pumps. Mick's soft brown hair would be intricately braided, interwoven with tiny pearls or specks of diamonds catching the light. A string of larger pearls, milky smooth on her upper chest, would pale by comparison to her own cameo complexion.

They would collar her, too, Thompson or the men who bought her for the night. A black velvet choker with a many-faceted stone to mark her as theirs, though to no avail. At dinner, the theater, the club, Mick would be the most beautiful woman there and while she might wear their mark she could never be owned, not at any price.

"You are a most imaginative man." Mick's subdued murmur brought me back.

"I am?" Good thing my fantasy hadn't gone much farther.

"I surmise that you are, yes. We were speaking. You became distant. I presumed it to be quixotic contemplation. A romantic hides behind your many walls, Kim Murayama."

"You think so, huh?"

The barest inkling of a smile touched her lips. "I am quite certain of it, yes."

Any streak of romanticism I harbored ran as a deep undercurrent in a river of guilt. Romance bled to death in a snow-covered alley years ago. My chest tightened and I fully expected to hear yet again how it wasn't my fault, but Mick didn't assail the walls.

"You will come out," she said quietly. "When it is time." She slipped an arm through mine as the *Lady* turned south between twin break-walls, making for the Welland Canal.

DAVE AND O'CONNOR WENT ashore to take care of the formalities – paperwork with a little grease if it was needed to help things along. Canada doesn't much care about a boat like the *Lady* as long as the informal conventions are observed. The lights of St. Catherine flickered to life and from astern a CZ-registered freighter approached. Dirty from bow to stern, rusted and streaked, she rode high, probably up-bound for a load of Central Zone corn or wheat. A few of her crew were on deck, dirty like their boat. They looked sneaky without even trying.

Rusted and streaky, dirty and sneaky. I grinned to myself. Too long to paint on the fantail, but fitting. Mick emitted a small giggle and immediately darted an apprehensive glance at me. I arched an eyebrow. "What's so funny?"

"Will you be angry if I say rusted and streaky and dirty and sneaky?" She wrinkled her nose. "You were thinking quite strongly."

"Like when I was wondering if you were immortal?"

"As when you were wondering about pearls."

Shit. "I was, but- you'd look good in pearls, by the way. But I was also wondering about immortality. Before it started to rain and got cold all of a sudden."

"Before we went below and you did not want to sleep with me."

"Yes," I groaned. "Then."

"I explained this to you." And it was as ambiguous an explanation as I'd ever heard. Mick laid a hand on my arm. "Do you still think me a witch, Mr. Murayama?"

She certainly wasn't a monster, but after all I'd seen… "I guess maybe I do," I said ruefully.

"I see." Mick offered no more. She turned to the rail and laid her head on my shoulder. Despite my unsatisfied curiosity and the attendant trepidation, I didn't move until Dave and O'Connor returned in the last fading twilight. When he saw Mick and I at the rail, her head still on my shoulder, Dave arched a mildly disapproving eyebrow, but didn't say anything. O'Connor didn't say anything, either, just grinned.

We cast off, easing into the canal for the trip to Lake Erie. A Canadian-flagged cabin cruiser that had also come in off Lake Ontario joined us. The *Lady* led into Lock 1, followed by the cabin cruiser and leaving the CZ freighter to wait its turn. Seaway workers dropped yellow lines from 50 feet above; I looped mine around a stern cleat, O'Connor taking the bow. We dragged the lines across the deck to the port side, farthest from the wall, allowing us the leverage to pull ourselves in as we rose and keep snug to the wall. Dave stayed at the helm as we repeated this process at each lock. By the time we "climbed the mountain," the twin flight locks 4, 5 and 6 at Thorold taking us up some 200 feet, it was full night. Coming out of Lock 7 O'Connor wandered aft, taking stock of things and finding Mick and me at the starboard rail. "Coffee on below," the big Irishman told us. "Just made."

"Thanks." I waved as he moved off. I was in no hurry, oddly content to stay right where I was next to a gal I should have been anxious to lose. Maybe it was wishful thinking, another chance to grab the brass ring as though I rode the long lost merry-go-round at the old amusement park. St. Catherines slid slowly astern, lights fading, leaving the stars free to shine in a moonless night sky.

Mick pointed overhead at Ursa Major. "Look. The Great Bear. The handle of the dipper is his tail. Have you ever seen the Horse and Rider?" She edged closer that I might sight along her outstretched arm. I did, inhaling the faint scent of northern pine in her hair. "The middle star in the handle. It is the Horse. The faint star close by... you see it?"

I squinted. "Yeah." I'd never noticed it before.

"It is the Rider. It was once a test of the eye. If you can see the Rider your vision is good."

I guessed I wasn't blind then. I pointed to Vega, bright in Lyra. "You know that one?"

"Uh, huh. The Harp Star."

I nodded. The Spinning Damsel, a Chinese version of Orpheus and his harp. I gazed up at the flickering point of light, recalling Master Shiyro relating the mythological tale under a similar sky, how the young man Tung Yung sold himself into slavery to afford his father a proper funeral. Seeing that the hardships nearly killed him, the Lord of Heaven took pity and sent his daughter Chih Nu to earth to rescue Tung Yung. They lived together for some time, he working in the rice fields while she cared for their house and wove incredibly beautiful silk tapestries at her loom. The tapestries brought them wealth to buy their freedom, but in the end Chih Nu had to go back to heaven. If the gods live as mortals too long they're no longer gods. She's there now, at her loom in the sky weaving tapestries for the gods. A sad story with more than one meaning for me. I kept those meanings to myself.

Mick pointed low to the east, at Andromeda. "The Chained Woman. And there Perseus who rescued her." She pointed again. "His magical horse flies. You are like Perseus."

Not hardly. If I was, Joanna would still be alive, weaving tapestries. "I'm not that much of a hero, Mick."

"Then that one." She gestured to another line of stars strung out above Polaris reaching to near zenith. "Draco suits you, I think. Dragons are the substance of legend."

"They're not real."

"Nevertheless." She laid a fingertip on my chest. "You rescued me. And you have the heart of the dragon." I smiled despite myself. She deserved her own constellation. She was as beautiful as any star in the sky. I almost told her that, but kept it, too, to myself.

As we motored toward the last lock, the glare of powerful floodlights grew, an alien world of shining steel and harsh white concrete. It would drive back the night and dissolve the constellations as dawn burns off the mists of dreams and wishes. Mick shaded her eyes. "At home when the night is come the lake disappears and all is still. But here…"

"In the winter it's still."

"When the snow comes." Her gaze lifted. "The sky is changed then. The Great Bear is moved. The Dragon is on his head and the Spinning Damsel almost touches the earth." She gave me a hesitant smile both apprehensive and hopeful. "Perhaps when the Damsel is closer to earth, Joanna is near?"

"Her spirit's with those of her ancestors," I said, staring at her. I hadn't told her any of the meanings of that tale. "And she died in October."

"But there was snow. It was cold."

"Yes." I closed my eyes, drew a breath and held it. There was snow and it had been cold. The Dragon was on his head and the Spinning Damsel touched the earth. She reached down and took Joanna to heaven with her. I turned away to hide the tear. I'd sworn I wouldn't cry any more and I'd be damned if I'd do it in front of Mick.

She held my hand for a while, then gently pulled free. I stayed at the rail, watching her go. She padded a few steps, paused. Enveloped in the shadow of the superstructure, she turned. Her voice came subdued. "One day when evening is come and all is still, when only the stars see, you will stay with me, Kim Murayama." Then she was through the door and gone. I stared after her for several long seconds, then wandered across to the portside rail, the lights of Niagara Falls a distant glow on the eastern horizon, as feeble by comparison as the Sovereignty is to Canada. Closer on shore a cemetery crept by swathed in gloom, luminous tombstones canted sharply in high grass. I couldn't remember the name of the burial ground. O'Connor had told me before, but tonight I couldn't remember. The place made me think of Joanna, a graveyard of memories and cemetery dreams. I watched the leaning stones fall behind, then climbed the ladder to the bridge.

Dave had the helm. He glanced over his shoulder. "Hey. Murayama. Listen, I'm sorry if I was kind of hardass before. About my office and all."

"Don't worry about it. I guess you had the right."

"I guess I did. And I'm not worried about it."

"What I mean is, don't let it bother you that you went off the handle. That it could have damaged our friendship."

"I'm not too worried about that, either," he said. I hadn't figured he would be. Dave swallowed more coffee, squinting in the approaching blaze of Lock 8. "She *will* pay, won't she? The witch. I mean, what's your feel on it?"

"I think they'll make it good." Cash, check, money order. Credit. I had no idea how payment would be rendered, but my gut said they'd do the right thing. More important than the money, though, I wanted to get Mick back where she belonged. "Listen, Dave..."

I outlined Doc Fredericks' theory on telomerase, human trafficking and the search for life everlasting that wasn't in Texas or anywhere else, how the witches had been exiled to Isle Royale. I thought he ought to know what had gotten us into this fix. I kind of expected him to get steamed and accuse me of getting him into this predicament, but he heard me out and just clucked his tongue. "You think you ought to be sleeping with her?"

"I ain't sleeping with her," I protested.

He shrugged and grinned. "Maybe you ought to be. How long's it been?"

It was none of Dave's business, but I answered him anyway, unsure why. "A while," I replied tightly.

"I don't think you'd be betraying Joanna," he went on, disregarding the impropriety of broaching the subject at all. "I mean if you got close to somebody else. I don't think it'd hurt you any, that's all."

"Even if it's a Royale?"

"Yeah." Dave looked forward again. After a minute he said, "Immortality, huh?"

"God blessed never die, pal."

"Well, who knows? Anything's possible, I guess. But even if it is..." He lifted his cup, found it empty, and scowled into it. "Who the Christ wants to live forever?"

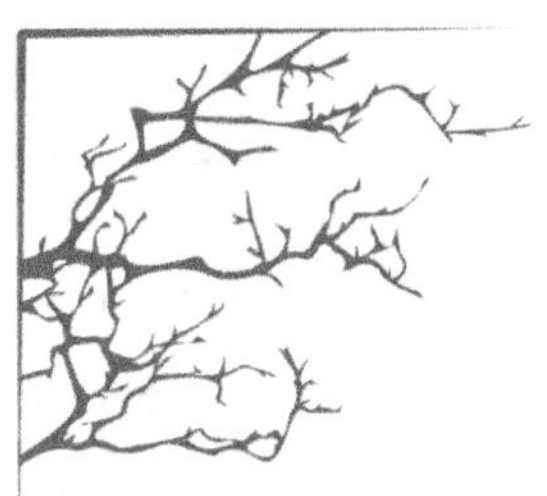

Chapter 5

After eleven hours in the Welland Canal we slipped easily beneath the Port Colborne lift bridge, leaving behind town homes, eateries and shops to pass warehouses, the grain terminal and docks of the city's thriving commercial marine district on our way to the South Outlet. Dave held the *Lady* on course, rounding the lighthouse and steering west as the first pink fingers of day felt their way over the horizon behind us. I made some breakfast in the galley – slab bacon from the cooler, cubed and boiled the way we used to do it in the Reserves, hard rolls and coffee. It's a long haul across Erie to the Detroit River and we'd all been up most of the night, so after everyone got something to eat I took the opportunity to catch up on some sleep. Mick smiled politely, if a little disappointed, when I left her at her own cabin. I was a little disappointed in myself, too, but crawled into my berth with my clothes on and fell asleep almost at once.

Another night was settling when I finally opened my eyes, blinking away the vestiges of an odd dream of running lost through a forest of balsam fir and white spruce. Nothing in the dream was familiar, but it left me oddly pensive. About what, precisely, was as elusive as the dream itself. I got up and went to the galley for coffee. The *Lady* had made good time and we were motoring up the Detroit River, already past the wreckage of the Ambassador Bridge, nothing more than twisted cables and bent spans hanging in the water. Mick was there, gazing out a porthole at the thick black smoke rolling slowly across the sky, blotting out the stars, shot through with the angry red and orange of the perpetual, uncontrolled fires raging across the ruins of Detroit, what remained of Dearborn, and beyond. She pressed her fingertips to the glass as if to touch Hell itself. "There are people there?" she whispered.

"Some." Not really people anymore from what I hear.

"The bridge fell into the river."

After Canada dynamited it. You can't blame them. After the Collapse – after the purgatory Detroit became – Canada was less concerned with international relations than they were with the starving, crazed inhuman inhabitants the survivors became getting across the bridge into Windsor. Upriver, Canada hasn't blown the 6000 feet of the Blue Water Bridge between Port Huron and Sarnia, but I understand it's wired and there's enough Canadian armor on the Sarnia side to make sure nobody gets to the Promised Land that way, either.

Eventually the smoke and stench dissipated as the ruined city fell behind. The *Lady* sailed to lee of Belle Isle, thence into Lake St. Clair. By the next dawn we were in Lake Huron. Dave held the *Lady* at 15 knots as we made for Sault Ste. Marie. As part of our fare Mick and I swabbed the main decks. This didn't involve scraping every foot with a hollystone and there wasn't any tar seeping from between the planks inasmuch as the *Lady* has metal decks, but we mopped them with lake water to remove the ash and grit from Dead Detroit. Taking a break, sitting propped against the superstructure, I worked a kink out of my shoulder. A pair of feet appeared beside me; I squinted up. Mick smiled through soot smudges. "I have finished my side. Do you require assistance?"

"Have a seat first." I patted the deck. We'd make the Soo Locks by the next night, then a couple days on Lake Superior and Mick would be home. I found myself troubled by the prospect of her leaving. She slid down beside me and crossed her legs. A warm breeze ruffled the faded blue denim shirt Dave had dug up for her. She'd tied it beneath her breasts, midriff bare, the gauze wrapping on her arm invisible under the long sleeve. I'd helped her change the dressing a few times; the wound looked to be healing well and didn't seem to much trouble her. "You'll be home soon," I said.

"And all will be well," she mused, looking off somewhere. "Except it will not. Thompson and men like him, heartless ones, they will continue to harass us." She pronounced it *hare-us*. Very proper.

I gazed into the distance, half searching for what she sought there and considering how it might be time the dealers in souls went out of business. Jo used to scold me for stuff like that, setting myself up as judge and jury. She said the world doesn't have to live up to my standards, that it's not my job to punish those who don't. I don't know as I see it as punishment. I'm not qualified to mete that out, but there's right in the world and there's wrong. Master Shiyro was always explicit about that. Everything's not black and white, no, but it's not all grey, either. Grey is the color of vagueness and Wrong loves that. It loves apathy and indifference. It lives with us in the shadows and whispers lies to confuse us. It grows stronger when we ignore it. There's right and there's wrong. You can tell one from the other. If you look. Maybe the Royales needed a champion who could see that.

Joanna used to say I have a hero complex, too, from listening to old man Shiyro, and I suppose I do, a little bit. But it's not much of a complex, like I'm not much of a hero.

Mick's fingertips brushed the back of my hand, feather light. She regarded me, head cocked. "What are you thinking?"

I gave her a crooked grin. "You tell me."

"Very well." She accepted the tacit challenge, the tip of her tongue peeking between her teeth. "Is it vengeance? No. Retribution, perhaps. For my sisters."

Maybe just for her. And maybe just for me. I put my head back against the cool steel of the superstructure, wondering if my psychological hero tendencies were getting out of hand again. Did the island really need a champion? Did they really need *me*?

"I need you," Mick whispered.

Mind reader, immortal witch, or just plain huckster, I liked hearing that from her.

THE *Lady* made the 300 miles from the St. Clair River to Sault Ste. Marie in just under twenty-four hours, taking the long route up the North Channel between Manitoulin and Cockburn Islands, then into Lake George, bypassing lake freighters and the larger, ocean-going salties using roomier Lake Nicolet below to enter the Saint Mary's River. We queued up for a quick transit of Canada's Sault Ste. Marie Canal above Whitefish Island, Dave at the helm. "Getting close," he said around his pipe stem.

"Yeah." I drank some coffee and stared at the gleaming double steel archways of the International Bridge over the four Sovereignty-operated locks.

"What if it's her evil wiles, Murayama?"

"What...? What if what is?"

"That idea you got of staying with her."

Dave knew me well. I *had* entertained the thought. Grabbing at the brass ring again on the merry-go-round of What Could Have Been. "A couple days ago you thought I ought to be in bed with her."

"A couple days ago I thought you were." Dave made a face. "But I been thinking. Maybe you better not screw her. Maybe those ideas you got about helping her or staying with her aren't yours."

"I ain't under any spell, man. That's fucking ridiculous."

"Then it's another vendetta. When are you going to quit avenging that poor dead girl?"

The world took on a sudden reddish tint; I ground my teeth. "Leave it be, Dave."

"All I'm saying is, you better not get wrapped up in this one. Not *this* one. We get my money and get out. Or I get out. You can stay if you want, but it's the money first. After that I don't give a flying fuck what you do."

I'd heard that before. At least he didn't mention anything about belated heroics.

Dave kept the throttles open and less than twenty-four hours later the prohibited Isle Royale came into view. A pair of heavy, powerful marine binoculars tight to his eyes, Dave scanned it across the expanse of Superior's cold waters. I leaned on the chart table, eyeing the green wax pencil line that marked our course from Whitefish Bay to a dead end in the middle of nowhere at the eastern tip of an island identified only by its thick red outline. *Stay Away. Nothing here.* Nothing and no one. Dave lowered the binoculars. "This the place, Miss Witch?"

Mick nodded impassively. "That is the Palisades. Duncan Bay is there."

Dave told O'Connor to bring the *Lady* about. We skirted a solid, rocky point sparsely sprinkled with Jack pine and turned into the mouth of a long bay stretching away to the southwest between fingers of forested land. We throttled back as it narrowed, Dave at the helm while O'Connor took soundings. The bay itself was about two miles long, bounded to starboard by a narrow strip of forested land studded with more of the same rock outcroppings. The land rose higher on the opposite shore, a tall, rugged ridge covered with timber stretching off out of sight. The forest here, primarily spruce, grew thick and green up to a narrow strip of brownish-white sand dotted with driftwood, the water remarkably clear. I opened a port-side window and inhaled deeply of fresh, clean air with a taste of rain to come. Midway down the bay Dave cut the engines and threw a switch; heavy chain sang and the *Lady*'s anchor splashed. "We'll take the skiff in," he said. "Come on, Liam."

They left Mick and I alone on the bridge. I sucked my teeth and looked at the deck. At my sneakers. I started to scuff one toe, but managed to curb the adolescent impulse.

Mick cleared her throat. "Thank you for bringing me home, Kim Murayama."

"You're welcome. It was... something." I was going to say it was nothing, but it was something. Meeting her had been something.

"Will you come ashore?" she asked, her tone betraying nervous hope.

"I guess. If you want."

"I very much want you to. I wish-" Abruptly she turned away, one hand to her mouth. When she turned back she'd recovered her composure, but I saw the moisture in her eyes. "There is nothing to be sad about, is there?" She took my hand. "Come. You have brought me this far. Take me the rest of the way home."

I obliged her and we headed to the main deck. O'Connor remained on board as the rest of us piled into the skiff. Approaching the shore the clouds thinned as Dave tilled the skiff with Mick and me in the bow. We held hands as the thick, dark pines drew near. Cleaned and mended, her loose black top fluttered in the gentle breeze.

"You would like the sunsets here," she told me. "They are agreeably slow. They do not hurry evening. When the sun sets and the night is finally come, when only the stars can see, then all is still." At that moment Dave ran the skiff aground. Mick clutched the thwart with one hand, the other gripping my arm with sudden, unexpected urgency. "Here is not at all like your great city!" she whispered fiercely. "Remember that!"

She bounded out, splashing in the surf while I sat scowling to myself until Dave shouted. "The bow line, Murayama! Get a move on!" I jumped into the water. Heavy, wet rope paid out behind me as I jogged up the sand and found a suitable white pine. Dave gave me thumbs up as he tramped ashore. Twenty yards down the beach a wary osprey perched on a dead limb hanging out over the water, hackles up as he scrutinized this interruption. Deeper in the forest among the sugar maples and a variety of firs, a woodpecker hammered unseen. Mick stood at the tree line by the opening of a narrow path, very much at ease in the environment.

Dave came up behind me. "Is she getting the money? Tell her to get my money and let's get out of here. This place gives me the creeps."

"The creeps?" Late afternoon sunlight sparkled on the bay, anything but sinister.

"We don't belong here and they don't want us." His hand went beneath his jacket, came out with the black .40 caliber. "They hate us. They're in the God damned trees."

I clutched his arm. Dave's forearm tensed like steel, knuckles white around the automatic's grip. He quivered, the gun pointing at the path's opening. Mick wore a horrified expression, her eyes beseeching me, but she said nothing as a distinguished lady, slim with silver-grey hair pulled severely back, led a small party onto the beach. She wore a long, hard grey cloak that matched her hair and eyes. The others, four young women about Mick's age, wore the loose black shirts and baggy black pants, each individually striking, and collectively stunning. One stood six feet or more, lithe and painfully beautiful with 18 karat golden-blonde hair matching liquid gold eyes with feline-slit pupils that shimmered above high cheekbones. Another stood as tall as Mick with a similar build, but her hair was a vibrant emerald green growing wild to her shoulders about a vaguely elfin face. Jade eyes glittered.

"Ho-lee shit," Dave breathed. His arm sank, lowering the pistol.

The third one had black hair so rich and lustrous it shone like blued steel in the afternoon sun. Black, intimidating flame smoldered in ebony eyes set in ghostly pale features, seizing me, almost pinning me. I barely tore free, doing so with an inexplicable reluctance, and stared at the fourth Royale.

A brunette like Mick, I swore for a moment it *was* Mick. She wore her hair down about the same oval face and creamy complexion, wide brown eyes promising equal intrigue. If she wasn't Mick's twin she'd damn sure do until the real thing came along. And yet I found myself less attracted to her – to any of them, as strangely enchanting as they were – than to Mick.

Mick bowed to the older woman, a good 45 degrees that we'd use at school to show great respect for Sensei. "Docent Edrea," she said courteously, almost deferentially.

"Mick." The woman inclined her head, but didn't reciprocate with a bow. "You have returned."

Mick took a half step back and gestured for Edrea's benefit. "This is Mr. Murayama and Mr. Hanson. From the great city. They have brought me home." She glanced at us. "Edrea, docent and counselor."

"Ma'am." I bowed. *Otagai ni rei* – bow to each other – and got the same nothing that Mick had received in return. I noted the barest hint of burned nutmeg or maybe cinnamon accompanied Edrea, unnatural amid all the nature. Dave gave a curt nod. If the pistol hanging by his leg gave Edrea or any of her retinue pause, they hid it well behind impassive expressions.

"Mr. Murayama. Mr. Hanson," Edrea murmured, "We are deeply in your debt."

Dave grunted. "How deeply?"

"Mr. Hanson was promised recompense," Mick averred. Edrea's expression remained placid.

"Indeed he was," Dave declared. "After his office burned down and people tried very hard to shoot him because he was associating with a Royale witch. If that's what you are. I really don't give a damn, but this was a lot of trouble, so you may compensate me plenty adequately."

"So we shall," Edrea allowed. "We cannot thank you enough. And you, Mr. Murayama?"

I waved the offer aside. "I don't need anything."

"Will you then, at least, accept our hospitality of the evening?"

Dave wasn't at all thrilled with the invitation to dawdle someplace we shouldn't have been at all, but the danger of discovery and apprehension appeared, frankly, minuscule. I argued that the Royales would need time to put together his sizable payment.

He shoved the pistol back under his jacket. "This better be quick, Murayama. I want to get out of here." He slapped at a mosquito, then lowered his voice. "They hate us. I want my money and I want to be gone. The yardarm won't go away."

"They don't *hate* us," I objected. Christ, we'd just been invited to dinner. Edrea turned and moved regally back up the path, her four retainers following. Mick stood to one side nibbling her lip anxiously.

"She's got you," Dave muttered. Swatting at more mosquitoes which didn't seem interested in me, he tromped after Edrea. "She's had you since the M."

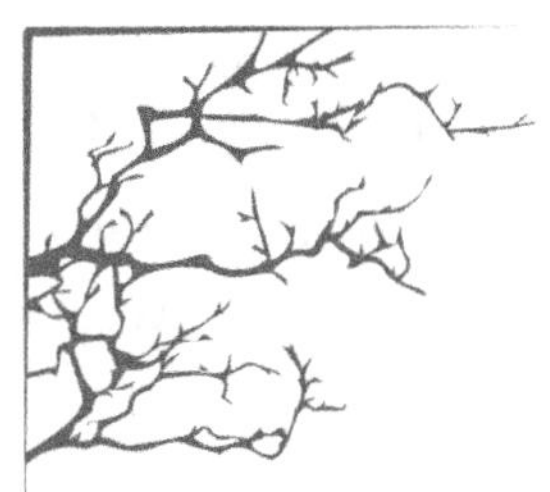

Chapter 6

Dinner sizzled on an open fire in a broad ring of stone, the aroma of trout skewered on sticks and the tang of wood smoke making me salivate. The Royales laid out loaves of fresh hearth-baked bread, cheese curd, fruit, and wine served in smooth wooden cups. I especially liked the raspberry wine. It was light red, a hint of sweet, smooth and relaxing as a bottled sunset. I had trouble imagining where all this provender came from on an isolated island. Some of it could be home grown, but it seemed to me some of it had to be imported. Canada, maybe. There didn't appear to be any blockade operating, so maybe. For the time being I filed away my curiosity, subject to recall.

The small crowd in the clearing grew. Most were women about Mick's age, all in comparable clothing, black or earthy brown in color, loose but neat. Comfortable. Here and there I spied a short cloak against an evening coolness off the water. Most of the Royales in attendance were brunettes like Mick, uniformly of a remarkable similarity in appearance. There were several golden-blondes, too, tall with a supple grace. I saw only one or two Royales with green hair and none of the pale ones with the jet black hair and the dark, mysterious eyes that had tried to trap me on the beach for unknown reasons. Some of them played somewhere nearby – stringed instruments and woodwinds above soft, simple drums, drifting around the murmur of quiet conversation and whispering pine boughs.

The few young men in attendance, mostly brunette as well with long hair in their eyes, and a couple poorly combed golden-blondes mixed in, kept to themselves, drinking and talking in hushed tones. I caught an occasional petulant glance my way. One of the blonde ones tried to stare me down. I accepted the challenge and eventually he looked away.

I spotted Mick on the opposite side of the fire, chatting with two other young women, a brunette and a blonde. I thought them not the same ones who had accompanied Edrea to the beach, though I couldn't be sure. The instant I thought of Edrea the hairs on the back of my neck stood up. I pivoted slowly and for a second my nose wrinkled at a fleeting scent so short lived that I wondered if I hadn't imagined it. She stood just beyond the firelight, wrapped in her grey cloak and the somber arms of forest night. She'd demonstrated her disinclination to return a respectful bow so I dispensed with the courtesy and gave her a nod this time, civil if not polite.

"Mr. Murayama. I trust you are enjoying yourself." I raised my cup in acknowledgment. After a reflective pause Edrea went on. "I must thank you again for returning Mick to us. Without you I doubt that we could have expected to see her again. Such affairs seldom have a favorable ending."

"Do they ever?"

One corner of her mouth quirked up. "On the infrequent occasions that one of us manages to make her way back, the experience nearly always proves to be of such nature that she is unable to reestablish herself." She meant that they didn't fit in any more. I swallowed some raspberry wine, watching her over the edge of the cup. She looked past me, to the fire where shifting shadows painted figures ocher and black. "We are different, Mr. Murayama. Our ways are different, ill-suited to the world you know. Any significant exposure is literally overwhelming. The contamination is irreversible."

And if they were sold by men without hearts? What happened to them then? Hardly had the thoughts formed than a sudden, gripping apprehension seized me. It sprang from the darkest abyss and took instant root. Mick could be affected!

No. She *was* affected. They *were* different. The Sovereignty was a disease, a contagious, deadly pestilence infecting everything and everyone. Mick had been taken there and it infected her as surely as any pathogen. I spun, searching, unable to find her. The fire moved, or the ground itself carried me. Faces slid past in shadow black or slashes of orange, angry faces with venomous eyes. Dave was right – they hated us as anyone would hate a cancer eating them. Killing them. I ran before they killed *me*, darting past or pushing aside dark shapes without feature and unreal. They'd gotten Dave already. They'd get O'Connor, too. Sink the *Lady*. If I didn't get off the island my fate was sealed, no one to ever know.

"Murayama! Whoa, lad. Whoa." Powerful hands gripped my biceps, lifted me off my feet and swung me round. I slammed an outside block right, then an inside block left, breaking both holds, and dropped snarling into a middle stance. "Ow! Christ Jaysus, boy. Stand down."

"O'Connor... ?"

"No. Saint Patrick, ye dolt." He frowned down at me, fists on hips.

"What are you doing here?"

"Having dinner. Dave give me leave to come ashore. Fish smells real fine, too."

I grabbed his shoulder. "They're gonna' sink the ship, Liam. The witches."

"They are not."

"They've killed Dave!"

"They've done no such thing. Get hold of ye'self."

Scowling, Dave stepped out from behind O'Connor. "What the hell's ailing you now, Murayama? Are you drunk again?"

I looked around for my missing wooden cup. "No. I ain't drunk."

"Then stop acting like a buffoon. Everybody's looking at you." He touched the elbow of a tall, lithesome blonde that might or might not have been the one I saw talking with Mick previously, and they moved off together, Dave murmuring, "I apologize. He's an idiot."

"Kim...?" Fingers touched my arm. I started, but relaxed with a sigh of relief. It was Mick. She smiled uncertainly, features glowing like burnished copper in rippling firelight. She held a dark, polished wood plate with some food. "You are uncomfortable."

I shot a look where Edrea had been; the forest stood deep and empty. "I was, uh, worried. I couldn't see you. I couldn't see Dave and I thought- look, I know this is crazy, but I thought you were going to kill us and sink the Lady."

"*Kill* you...?" She blinked in amazement.

"Before we infect you. Edrea told me what happens when you're taken from the island."

"Ohh. That." She affixed an overly sober expression. "I am not contaminated. See?" She stepped closer and whispered, "My world and yours, they did not touch so long. You understand?"

I wanted to. I wanted to understand everything and understood almost nothing. Mick smiled in the dancing firelight and took my hand. Balancing the plate she led me around the fire. More wood had been added; hot sparks swirled and twisted upward toward diamond bright stars burning in a velvet black sky. Mick drew me to a sheltered spot beneath overhanging pine boughs where Dave puffed on his pipe and reclined against a large piece of bleached driftwood next to the tall blonde Royale. Once he'd assured himself that I wasn't drunk, he introduced her as Sena. Yellow cat-eyes without emotion watched me as though stalking a bird at the feeder.

Having observed the social requisites under a fir tree, I dropped onto a log and stared into the flames, dimly aware of a mosquito's high-pitched whine near my ear, but then beating a hasty retreat. Mick sat beside me, plate balanced on her lap, and encouraged me to have some supper. The fish – trout, I judged – was a little greasy, but tender and mild, the bread and cheese tasting in all respects freshly made, and some type of small, round red berries with an uncommon tart-sweet taste. Music and singing continued. The green-haired Royale from the beach had reappeared and O'Connor danced with her, or tried to. Her attempts to instruct the big Irishman in some of the local steps met with mixed results. Mick leaned close, her shoulder touching mine. "I am pleased Mr. Hanson permitted Mr. O'Connor to come ashore. Shanna finds him most diverting."

"Shanna." I popped a piece of fish in my mouth.

"Uh, huh. She is from the Palisades near here. There are few of them."

"Do they, ah, all look alike, too? The way all the blondes look like each other. And the brunettes all look like you, Mick."

"You think I am like all the others." Her expression went flat. Too late I realized what I'd said. I backpedaled madly.

"You're not just like them, no. That's not what I meant. You're you, you know? You look like them – or they look like you – but you're not just like them. I don't think. I don't know anybody else, really, but I'm sure you're...unique." Backpedaling wasn't working. The chain was off the chain-ring, twisted up good in the derailleur. I wasn't going to be able to successfully shift gears and massaged my temples trying to forestall a stupidity headache.

Mick stared into the fire, brow furrowed. I'd said enough and kept my mouth shut. At length she inquired, "Do you truly find me more attractive than Jacqueline? She came to the beach with Docent Edrea and the others. She is a- she is like me. But you thought me the more attractive, yes?"

"I never said that."

"I know. Is it true?"

I let the thievery pass unremarked upon this time, maybe because she was right. I thought the brunette on the beach looked like her. I thought all the brunettes did, but I wasn't interested in them. I looked Mick straight in her brown eyes. "I'm interested in you."

She smiled shyly. "You are in no danger this night. You are not alone in dark forests with mysterious strangers who have lured you ashore in order to spirit you to your doom." Mick leaned close, her breast grazing my shoulder. Her lips brushed my ear. "Your secrets are safe with me, Kim Murayama, and I know mine are safe with you." Then she bounced off, returning shortly, another wooden cup brimming. We finished our meal, drank more raspberry wine and watched Shanna trying to teach O'Connor to dance. The job was too big; she called for reinforcements and several Royales joined in, laughing.

People came by to talk. I met Celia and Rachel, Miriam and Emma. Celia was blonde, tall and for all the world looking like Dave's companion Sena. The rest were brunette, each manifestly resembling one another and Mick. They inquired after Mick's adventure and spoke politely if superficially with me – How are you? Are you enjoying yourself? Do you like the fish? Thank you so much for bringing Mick home. Gracious but reserved. During our conversations I glanced about in search of the young male Royales from earlier. They were nowhere to be seen.

I did see the pale, raven-haired young woman who had come down to the beach with Edrea. She stood silently at the edge of the fire's illumination, on the border between light and shadow. We stared at each other and the voices around me dwindled, the air growing cool. The forest shifted behind her, becoming darker still, pushing firelight aside. I tried to move and couldn't. Her eyes bored into mine, black as pitch and lightless as a Stygian mine.

Run. Fly.

I came to my feet, but as quickly as she'd caught me she released her hold, drifting away with the smoke from the fire. I shivered and edged closer to the flames. She'd spoken in my mind, startling and disconcerting, not at all the way Mick had. Wood smoke mixed with pine and the familiar aroma of cherry tobacco, and for a fraction of a second my nose wrinkled at that peculiar "something else."

Burnt cinnamon. No doubt about it. I half expected to find some 'muted streeter off the Strip lounging against a blue spruce and sucking a stick, but the woods beyond remained empty. Sena sat next to Dave, long legs tucked beneath her. She spoke quietly and patiently, explaining something to him I couldn't follow. He glanced up at me, his pipe in one hand. "What's the matter now, Murayama?" He slapped at a mosquito.

"I don't know," I replied slowly. "What're you smoking in that thing?"

"Captain Black. Keeps the bugs away. It's not bothering you, is it? There's a God damned bonfire going, but I don't want my pipe offending you."

"No, it's not bothering me." I looked at Sena.

"That is of your world," she murmured, somewhere between explanation and accusation.

Contamination. I nodded to myself. Mick's friends had moved off and she stood studying me, head cocked to one side. After a moment she extended a hand. "Come. Walk with me."

I accepted and took her hand. I checked over my shoulder as we made our way around the fire, but there was no sign of the pale Royale and her penetrating, captivating obsidian eyes. We came to a fair-sized crowd laughing and clapping as O'Connor now attempted to instruct Shanna in the finer points of an Irish jig. We loitered on the periphery, hanging back by mutual consent. A few of the closest Royales glanced at us and smiled.

Mick squeezed my hand. "Something disturbs you."

Where to start. Stale smoke and cinnamon. Onyx eyes darker than midnight, a witch's spell of smoke and moonlight. I wanted to know who that one was. "When we first got here on the beach there was a gal. Black hair, with Edrea."

"That was Aimee. She is from the far end of the island where the winds blow. She customarily prefers to remain apart. She is solitary. They all are. I do not believe she is here."

She had been, though, telling me to run. To fly. I probably *should* have run. The island's prohibited. I was trespassing. And there was the question of penance. I promised Joanna.

"Forever?" Mick asked quietly.

I didn't reply. I didn't know the answer. In the trees and night the music slowed; deep, unhurried woodwinds resonated, foundation for a single haunting voice. It came from a distance, spirit-song carried on winds across the water. Other voices joined in, retreated, reappeared and retreated again.

Shifting shadows danced through darkened pines filled with strange, compelling music that moved magically closer. I gazed at Mick, at lovely mystery and the most beautiful unknown. The music faded to silence stretching for several seconds. The fire crackled. Someone murmured indistinctly and then a solitary tubular bell rang dulcet in the night. Mick's ears pricked up. The chime faded, replaced by a susurration of voices. The bell rang again, the susurrus resurrected and a hidden dulcimer's strings took the lead above a hollow, impelling drumbeat. Shanna appeared from nowhere, eyes flashing jade bright. "Mick!"

"Yes!" Mick quivered, fists balled tightly at her sides. She fixed me for an instant, then spun and scampered to where the singers and musicians gathered. Their music swelled anew, exotic, unfathomable words mixing with shadow and firelight. Expression dreamy, Mick swayed with the rhythm possessing the night. History and magic came alive, wonderful folklore and fabulous mythology woven incorporeal and inescapable through the trees, in the very air. Mick's hands came up, shoulders shifting gently; her hips moved, feet sliding subtly and softly in an alluring physical manifestation of the spellbinding musical energy. When the first chorus ended she, too, began to sing.

The others deferred to Mick. Her eyes opened and her gaze fastened on me. She sang angelic, in perfect concert with dulcimer and drum, with chiming bell and sweet refrains. She sang to me in a language I didn't comprehend, yet somehow I understood. Everyone heard, everyone saw, but the song was only for me. Surrounded by the music, held by her words, I stood again on crumbling ledges above rocky shores, a featureless world of grey days jumbled upon grey days, outside Joanna's mausoleum in a cold, soulless wind plucking at the last tattered scraps of memory. Mick stood with me. Carefully, she opened the door to that dark, dusty place. She could have entered, could have forced me within, but instead she slowly closed the door leaving memory undisturbed unless I chose otherwise.

Then I was back by the fire. The music crescendoed to its climax, ending much too soon with the final echo of the tubular bell fading into night as it had begun. Mick bounced over, expression anxious and hopeful. Her friends smiled; some laughed, others clapped soft approval. She stood on her toes, slightly breathless, to kiss me.

Later, as the fire died and people drifted away by twos and threes, Mick led me to a cedar-shingled, saddle-notched log cottage in the woods. She knew the way through the magic forest. If there were lamps, we didn't use them. Moonlight crept in, blue-white on the straw and clay-plastered walls. We touched, gentle as that delicate veil while distant angel voices whispered through the pines.

"I have never sung that song for anyone before," she breathed. Her palms rested on my chest. "It was for you." Her lips brushed my ear. "For us."

I closed my eyes, my hands on her waist. I kissed her forehead, her hair, and Mick drew me to the bed.

"Only the stars see now, Kim Murayama. Evening is finally come and all is still."

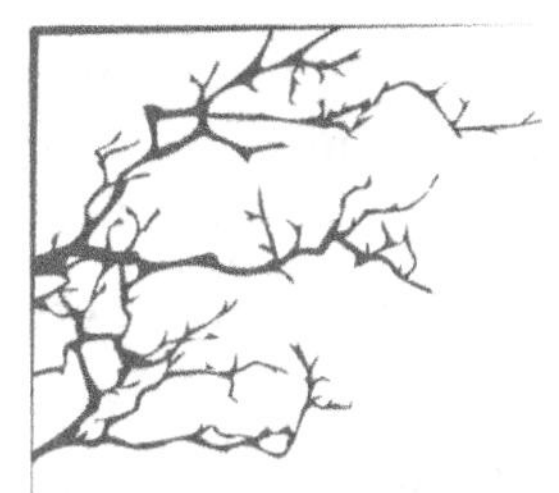

Chapter 7

With the sun barely peeking over the window sill I slipped from under the covers, careful not to wake Mick, and stood on cool, smooth plank flooring dappled in early morning's light. Mick's breath came softly, her chest rising and falling gently beneath a brown wool blanket. Soft and composed, her features betrayed nothing but serenity. I couldn't tell if we had a future here in the woods, but the prospect was more attractive than ever.

I dressed and let myself out of the bedroom, scanning the spartan furnishings I'd missed the night before – small, simple round dining table with rough-cut Shaker legs and hardened wax drippings on top, two simple ladder-back chairs, a wooden washtub on a sideboard against one wall. The window panes were that wavy type of glass, with no curtains. Spartan, but appealing. I slipped out the front door, catching a glimpse of a narrow, rough-hewn outbuilding in the trees behind the cottage. Investigation revealed it to be a pit toilet – a one-holer – stocked with carefully sized white squares of what I thought might be flour sack cloth and a dented bucket in the corner for its disposal. Rudimentary, but, as I discovered, sufficiently functional.

The day already grew warm as I passed the remains of the previous night's bonfire and made my way down to the beach. Despite little sleep I felt invigorated. I intended to stretch out, maybe perform a few slow kata and rinse off in the bay, but I found Dave sitting at the edge of the woods not far from the empty skiff. Further out, the *Lady* waited patiently, tickled by morning's mists. Dave looked up, cold pipe in one hand. A small black cloth bundle lay on the ground between his feet. He squinted at me. "Have a good time last night?"

"Pretty good. Bet there's more than one cottage tucked away in the woods."

Dave chuckled. "A-yeah, there is. But listen. That song Mick sang? You know what it means?"

"I think it was kind of a love song."

"Kind of, yeah. It's a declaration, buddy. She as much as told everyone there last night that you're engaged. Sena said when a Royale sings that song to someone, it's because she's picked him." I looked around, at lazy clouds in a bright sky, the bay stretching off toward Lake Superior, and wondered how often contrabands confined to their island got to sing it to anyone at all. Dave fiddled with his pipe. "Sena says it's not done with outsiders, although in your case it's probably especially bad taste."

I tried not to sound porky. "You think I'm not good enough for Mick?"

"I don't know how good you'd be for anybody, Murayama. And speaking of Outside..." He used his toe to push the black cloth bundle toward me. I retrieved it, peeled a fold away to find eight dark green rough cut gems, the largest about as big as my thumb, the others smaller but still good size.

I held up one oblong shape. It wasn't polished by any means, but its rich facets attracted the eye nonetheless. "Emeralds...?"

"Greenstones. My compensation. Worth, oh, three, four thousand apiece, I'd guess." He took the stone from my hand and tossed it back with a clink. "But you know what? These fucking things might's well be down in South America as in my hand."

Not knowing much about gemstones I would have thought Dave well compensated at thirty thousand B worth of emeralds. I'd've been dead wrong and he let me know it.

Emeralds aren't native to the Great Lakes region any more than diamonds are; they don't belong on Isle Royale any more than we do and they ought rightly to be down in South America. If Dave went asking that kind of dough for a shitload of something that must be somebody else's, and that he presumably didn't come by all that legally, there'd be a hard look taken and quite possibly a rope over the yardarm. The Royales couldn't have picked worse tender if they'd tried. I eased down next to him, propped my chin in one hand. "So what're you gonna' do?"

"I dunno." He flopped back on the sand and stared at the pale blue sky. A lone gull wheeled overhead. "Maybe put in somewhere before we hit the M, swap one or two for C-bills. Selling a couple in Canada might not attract too much attention."

"Well, there you go. You can slide up before you head home."

"What? You staying? Jesus, Murayama." Dave scowled at me as though I was the biggest idiot in Lake Superior. "Are you really as stupid as you look?"

Neither Yes or No as an answer made me look anything but. "I meant we." It was a Freudian slip. Must have been.

Just then O'Connor ambled from the trees, one big arm draped affectionately around the much smaller green-haired Royale's shoulders. "Morning, boys. Were ye enjoying ye'self last night, Kim?"

"Well, I was until just recently." I hopped to my feet and brushed off my pants.

"Do you intend to spurn her?" Shanna was suddenly in front of me, jade eyes demanding. "Mick sang for you. You understand what that means?" She peered closely. "Yes, very well. As you do."

It was no God damned wonder they were quarantined. I excused myself and headed for the trees, O'Connor's good-natured laughter rippling in my wake. Apparently his one night stand wasn't complicated by the same encumbrances as mine. I walked along the path, head down, thoughts crowded with insistent memory of alien words in an indecipherable song, of firelight and wonder, moonlight and hope. I almost walked right into six feet of blonde Royale. I managed to avoid running into her, barely. She gazed down at me, eyes glittering like sunlight off gold. "Mr. Murayama."

"Sena, isn't it?" It could have been her twin, though deep down I knew it wasn't. I hooked a thumb over my shoulder. "Dave's on the beach."

"I am looking for you. Are you returning to Mick? Surely you cannot mean to spurn her. She sang for you."

"I know." I edged around her. "If you'll excuse me." That predatory feline gaze bored into my back as I hurried on. The whole island watched me. I hunched my shoulders and kept going until I found Mick on the front step of the cottage, chin in her hands. She wore black shorts and a loose black top that seemed a perfect match with her dark, doleful mien.

"Kim. Good morning. I thought you perhaps gone."

"Spurning you?" I might as well have slapped her. She looked away, tight-lipped. I sat down beside her and massaged my brow. "I'm sorry, Mick. That was uncalled for."

"You are under no obligation." Her voice was brittle. I wasn't from her island so the song had no meaning. She refused to look at me.

"It's not that way, Mick. I know what it means and I'm glad you sang for me."

She shifted, finally looking at me with moist eyes. "Are you? Last night I thought yes, but now I am uncertain."

I nodded mutely. I didn't want to leave, but could I justify staying? The dealers in souls ought to be opposed, yeah, but did she really need my help or did I just need to play hero to make up for something that could never be set right? Mick had escaped the M, she was home. That should be enough. If it wasn't... well, no amount of heroics would change the past.

"Who was she?" Mick's voice, almost inaudible, roused me. "Will you not tell me? I do not know your world, but I would at least understand the one small part of it that has touched my heart. I would understand you, Kim Murayama."

I nodded slowly. If she really wanted to know...

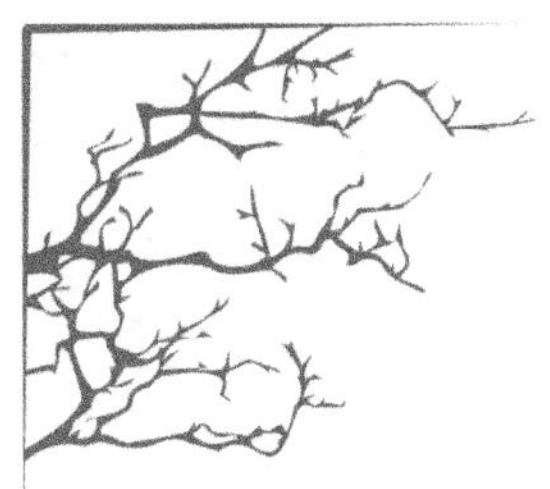

Chapter 8

A light snow fell the morning I left for Elmira – Hellmira, the troops called it; the nickname's not original, but it still fits. It was a Thursday in October, the snow an early one that wouldn't last. Joanna walked me to the armory, wet flakes glistening on her smooth, jet black hair. She had it tied in a long ponytail falling over her shoulder, rather more occidental and contrasting with her almond-shaped eyes. Her father Myin Rei was full-blooded Japanese, her mother of undetermined North American stock. Mr. Rei tolerated my courtship of his daughter inasmuch as we had, somewhere back there, a common heritage. He didn't care much for soldiers even though I was Reserves and almost out of the Combat Services, and he made it clear I'd better be about something more respectable if I fancied his daughter's hand. I always got the impression he didn't think much of my training at Master Shiyro's, either, though he never mentioned it in as many words.

We said our good-byes outside the brown block-stone armory, it being too noisy inside with trucks idling and troopers hollering. We were going for two weeks of garrison and picket duty, but we had tons of equipment to haul, supplies for almost 800 men, and several pieces of light artillery.

"Two weeks?" Joanna's teeth indented her lower lip the way she always did when she was worried and didn't want to say so.

"Two weeks, JoJo," I assured her. That's all we were scheduled for, just to relieve the 13th for some R&R. Unless something big happened. No one expected anything would. She smiled, a brave attempt to act casual. I think now it was a premonition, but back then I had no idea. How could I have?

The 1st Sergeant caught sight of us through the open overhead door and gave me a shout to get a move on. Several of the guys in the company were stowing gear in a 2X and started hooting and waving at Jo. She blushed and lowered her eyes the way she always did. I lifted her chin with a finger. "I love you, Jo."

"I love you, too. Always." She rose on her toes and gave me a quick kiss. A moment later she was scampering up the walkway, ponytail bouncing. She turned to wave. I gave her thumbs-up and watched her all the way up to the intersection. She waved once more before disappearing around the corner.

It was the last time I ever saw Joanna Rei.

SOMETHING DID HAPPEN. Six days after we assumed picket duty the bandits hit all over the province in the largest offensive they'd ever undertaken. Even though it turned out they weren't organized under any kind of central command, the initial attacks seemed incredibly well coordinated and were extremely successful. There had been no intelligence even hinting at this. It scared the Sovereignty badly.

We fought for almost a week, clearing them out of settlements and chasing them back into the deep wastes. After mopping up and burying the dead, theirs and ours, it was closer to four weeks by the time we loaded up and rolled north. I'd written Jo two or three times without receiving any letters back. I wrote her again explaining what happened, but by then it didn't matter.

After we unloaded I went straight from the armory to the bakery, lugging my duffel on my shoulder through a cold rain. It was Tuesday, about 2:00 o'clock. Jo would be at the store. I pushed through the door, the little bell overhead tinkling as my uniform began to drip on the floor. From behind the counter Dana looked up, color draining from her face. Her lips moved, but nothing came out. I frowned. "Is Jo here?"

Dana still couldn't speak. Kelly appeared through the swinging door to the kitchen, arms loaded with loaves of bread. She went as white as Dana; loaves bounced off the floor and one hand went to of the counter to steady herself. "Kim. Ohh, Jesus, Kim, I'm sorry."

Dana dug in her apron, producing a letter. She held it out, hand shaking so badly the envelope rattled. Heedless of the flood I was creating I crossed the shop floor, combat boots squishing, and took the letter. It was the last one I'd written Jo, telling her. It was still sealed. She'd never opened it. Tears streamed down Kelly's cheeks and it all came out in a rush, as confusing to me now as it was that late afternoon in the rain.

Jo was dead, died the day I left for Elmira. Something about the armory, the police, a funeral... Dana's face in her hands, sobbing something. I couldn't hear her. Kelly was speaking, trying to hand me a small bundle of letters, and I couldn't hear her, either. It was hard to breathe. The shelves closed in on me and I fled into the rain. Kelly ran after me, crying and calling, but I couldn't understand her. Maybe she was trying to tell me that I'd left my duffel bag, but I didn't care. I couldn't hear traffic. I did hear the little bell over the door when I left, the last time I ever heard it, but nothing else. I didn't feel the rain or the cold. I ran up the walkway and across the street, and then I don't know where. I ran until I couldn't run any more. When I couldn't run, I walked, staggering drenched and bedraggled. Eventually it was dark and I found myself at our apartment. I went upstairs, soaked to the bone, still feeling nothing.

The apartment was empty. Not just unoccupied, but empty the way a place is after a lovely spirit has flown never to return. That was when I finally felt the cold.

MR. REI EMPTIED THE apartment. Most of the things belonged to Jo anyway, but there was one thing I wanted. A keepsake. I loved the woman. We were going to marry. It was a mistake, but I went to see him.

Mrs. Rei answered the door. She lowered her eyes and stepped aside, overtly formal, stilted to the point of rudeness. Previously she hadn't disapproved of me. I went to the living room and bowed to Mr. Rei. He didn't even get out of his chair and spoke with barely controlled anger. "They killed her, Murayama. Good for nothing, no account shit that hangs out around that God damned armory!" Now he came out of the chair, fists clenched. "That slum! Barrooms and brothels and nothing good! My daughter should never have gone there. You never should have *let* her go. She died because you took her down there!"

If he had attacked me he would have won easily. I hadn't the heart to offer even a token defense. All that Shiyro taught me and I couldn't have raised a finger against him. But he didn't. He didn't even yell any more, just told me to get out. Mrs. Rei saw me to the door. She kept her eyes lowered. I asked about Jo's things. There was a bracelet, a copper band with our names inscribed. Mrs. Rei shook her head. There had been no bracelet. Jo had been robbed. Nothing was left. I'd troubled them enough and took my leave.

Later I found out what happened.

A SONGBIRD TRILLED and an errant breeze stirred Shiyro's white beard as the old master sipped bitter green tea and eyed me across *chabudai*. The low, black lacquered table had been brought out and placed near the small fountain in the courtyard. Normally you'd find this table inside on tatami mats or even hardwood flooring, but placing it in the courtyard, especially in good weather, wasn't unheard of. Not as traditional, maybe, but things change. At length he asked, "What will you do now?"

"I dunno." I gave a listless shrug. The funeral was over. I'd missed it, being still down in the Wastes. Mr. Rei probably would have barred me anyway. He blamed me for his daughter's death. He'd hardly want to see me at the rites.

"She was a lovely girl," Shiyro said.

"Yes, Sensei. She was."

"Drink your tea," he murmured. "Then go to temple."

I went to temple then and many more times, praying to my ancestors, to the spirits, to God... anyone I thought might listen. Maybe they heard me, maybe they didn't. Nothing ever changed. Joanna's ashes blew on the four winds and whoever killed her was still out there. The police arrested no one. I stayed at the school, practiced every day, cleaned to earn my keep. I led a class now and then.

I went to the alley where it happened, too. Master Shiyro accompanied and stood with me. There wasn't much to see. Jumbled trash cans and dark pools of stagnant water. Rusted fire escapes, steps to nowhere, hung vulture-like above metal doors scarred like black tombstones splashed with blood – hieroglyphics of the day staking out the turf of the Resurrected Dead Men gang. It smelled of refuse and rubbish left too long, of decay that would never be reversed. An unfriendly place, it probably looked a little cleaner in winter, after a fresh snowfall, say. Studying flaking brown iron rungs and mildewed brick walls,

I wondered if anyone beyond those silent doors had heard anything. Done anything. If they'd bothered to look up. I wondered if they'd even noticed Joanna's blood the following morning. Probably not. The snow would have melted, the remnants of life and the stains of death running together unnoticed into the gutter. If anyone had bothered to look.

We stayed awhile, but I got no feeling of anything I could put into words, certainly nothing that brought me any comfort. I don't know as anything at that time would have. I don't think I wanted to be comforted.

When I wasn't at the school I started hanging out in bars and pool halls near the armory. I'd nurse a beer for hours, watching and listening. Eventually I heard stories about some lakers off the *Lawrence Brown,* stories about a couple of them in particular.

"They likes the women," an old bar fly told me one night as I leaned next to him, foot propped on the brass rail. He had the look of an old oiler or engineer, a man who knew the lakes, the boats and of what he spoke. "All a'time bothering the girls. If there ain't any in here, they bothers Syl." He shot a rheumy look at the woman tending bar.

Syl worked a rag around inside a glass. "Right enough. But I guess I can handle 'em. You want another drink, Ev?" The old engineer nodded grimly. She gave me a questioning look.

"I'm okay." My mug was still half full. When she returned with Ev's beer we talked some more. It'd been three or four weeks since she'd seen these men, maybe another three, four before that. Ev agreed, eyes fixed on that world that exists on the other side of the mirror in every bar room. Shipping season was coming to an end, most of the iron boats off the lakes or heading that way. The men probably wouldn't be back until next year. Still, I had a feeling.

It wasn't much trouble to find them. An afternoon visit to the docks and I knew the *Lawrence Brown,* registered out of Chaumont Bay, was expected within the week, downbound on her last run of the season.

Shiyro came to my room as I prepared. "What are you going to do, Kim?"

"I'm going to balance the books, Sensei."

"You are not a bookkeeper."

"It's part-time work." I shrugged into a denim jacket and picked up four star-shaped shuriken. Light glinted on razor sharp steel points.

"Vengeance is not yours to take," he cautioned. "The spirits will see justice done."

"Really?" I glared at him. None of this was his fault, but he was right in front of my anger and frustration. "I been asking them about that, but so far they ain't done much." They say justice comes in its time, but I was tired of waiting.

Shiyro could have stopped me, but he made no move. All he said was, "This is not the way, Kim. You dishonor the spirits. They will see justice done. Even to you."

I ignored him and marched out, the throwing stars secreted in a special pocket sewn inside the left front of my jacket.

THE *Lawrence Brown* was punctual, tying up in the cool night air. I loitered in the shadows of a corrugated steel warehouse, eyeing the broad, dark hull rising up from the quay. With a black knit watchcap and the denim jacket I looked enough like a laker to escape notice. I didn't need to fool anyone for very long.

In due course the crew disembarked for their liberty, loud and raucous, feet heavy on the gangplank. Two especially loud bruisers stood out, backslapping as they left the ship. It was them. I don't know how I knew, but I knew. I kept a discreet distance and followed them to a bar near the armory. I didn't have to wait long. They emerged more boisterous than before, lumbering down the street accosting such passers-by as they encountered, looking for the right mark the way they had the day I left for Elmira. I knew that when it was finished I'd find Jo's bracelet on one of them.

I trailed them to other bars, dogged them until, stinking drunk, they stumbled up an unlighted alley to relieve themselves. I followed, unbuttoning my jacket. It wasn't the same alley, but it looked and smelled the same. Garbage, urine... everybody's dump, everybody's toilet. Some peoples' playground. Tonight it was *my* playground. There was no new fallen snow to melt and carry away the stains, which I regretted, but it didn't stop me. From inside the concealed jacket pocket I drew two shuriken, held them lightly, one in each hand between thumb and forefinger. I watched the two men, dark shapes within shadows. I smelled their piss. One of them groaned softly as he went.

"Hey." I caught them both with their cocks in their hands. Their heads came round; they saw me, but too late. The shuriken flew silently from underhand throws, embedding themselves in quick succession with barely a muffled sound. I got one man in the left eye, his companion in the right, each blade passing through the Gateway to the Brain. I did it the way master Shiyro taught me – swift, quiet, complete. It was over in seconds. No one saw. They never had a chance to scream, but it wasn't instantaneous. They had enough time to realize what was happening, to look at me from one dying eye and know. It gave them time to be afraid before they died, as Joanna must have been.

They succumbed in a couple of heartbeats, but they had time to be afraid.

I crouched and pulled the shuriken free, wiping the stained blades on one man's pant leg, the other's sleeve. Then I stood and watched their blood drain, steaming soundless in the dank air. It soaked their clothing with dark stains, then ran invisible onto the dirty ground.

I wished there had been snow.

"YOU KILLED THEM." MICK'S dispassionate assertion held no trace of judgment.

"I did." Right or wrong, I did.

"They were the men you sought?"

They didn't have the bracelet. I searched them both, rifling their pockets like some desperate ghoul out of a graveyard, and didn't find it. I've never been 100% certain I didn't kill the wrong men that night. The spirits know my doubts, too. I think that's why I dream about Jo. Part of my penance, cemetery dreams. She wouldn't have wanted to be avenged. She wasn't that sort of person.

"Are you?" Mick asked gently.

"I was once," I replied, not caring that she knew. How she knew.

"And now?"

"I don't know." I squinted up at blue sky through the pines, then at her. "You've heard the story. What do you think?"

"I think you are a different man than the one in the story." Mick rose and smiled wistfully. "Would you like some breakfast? I have blueberries."

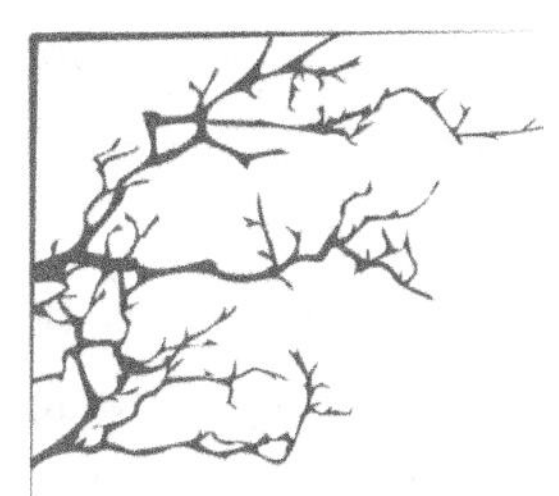

Chapter 9

I didn't leave right away. None of us did. Mick and I occupied the spare but cozy two-room cottage near Duncan Bay – I gathered it was community property of a sort, the larder minimally but sufficiently stocked. There were a couple of wooden buckets for water which I retrieved from Duncan Bay as necessary, and a small box wood stove on which Mick boiled rice and desiccated vegetables. There were hard bread crackers, too, but more often than not someone came by with fish or fresh bread, picked berries and home-grown garden vegetables. Some nights there would be a fire where Mick first sang to me and we'd have visitors.

I met Fern and Glynn, both from the nearby Palisades, both with Kelly-green hair and jade eyes, twin as twins can be. Several were brunettes from the central part of the island, hilly country I was given to understand, between Washington Creek, Sugar Mountain, and Hatchet Lake bounded by the Minong Ridge to the north and Greenstone Ridge to the south. Emma could have been Mick's twin. She visited several times, cooked fish on the fire and once drew a rough map in the dirt to show me where she lived near Little Todd Harbor on the north shore. She told me how in times gone by men took fish from the lake, metal from the ground and trees from the forest. I asked her if she'd always lived there.

She gave me an odd look. "Of course."

"Have you ever been off the island?"

"It is not permitted."

"Lots of things aren't permitted," I observed. "They happen anyway."

"What are you suggesting, Mr. Murayama?"

"Just asking."

"You ask many questions."

I guess I did. For instance, I hadn't seen any kids on the island. Hadn't seen any couples that would have children, frankly. Emma said the younger Royales were at Desor, near the lake, a boarding school type of thing as best I could determine. And The Boys, the fellas at dinner the other night who didn't seem real happy?

"You think they were disconsolate?" Her vocabulary was on par with Mick's, but otherwise she demurred. "I do not know what might anger them. I am sorry." I didn't find out where they were and politely didn't crowd the subject.

Most days Mick and I hiked Greenstone Ridge, the backbone of the island, sometimes playing tag around the Jack pine and white spruce or exploring the innumerable small paths branching from it. Traffic sounds, exhaust fetor, ceaseless movement – the closeness and apprehensive restlessness of the M itself – were all absent on Isle Royale, left behind in a world that, if I stayed here just a little while, I could easily forget.

One day we hiked a good distance, dropping southwest via what Mick called the Daisy Farm trail that took us to Rock Harbor and Moskey Basin along the eastern side of the island. We rested on a large rock outcropping near the collapsed and overgrown remains of some simple wooden shelters from another time. A cottontail rabbit poked its head out of the tall grass, nose twitching curiously.

I leaned back and stretched my legs, studying a slightly canted, forgotten lighthouse on a small spit of land across the water. The beacon's roof stood perhaps 50 or 60 feet above the water, capped with copper sheet gone a heavily weathered green. The whitewash on the tower and attached caretaker's house was little more than residue on the stone-and-brick construction, as faded as the island's past.

"A house of light," Mick told me. "Where the light does not shine." She was looking toward the lighthouse, but I thought beyond it, across the waters to some far, unattainable horizon. I was pretty sure she meant something else.

Not too far down the beach and near a well-maintained dock sat a concrete block warehouse-type structure built into a slight rise in the ground and painted a pale green under black asphalt shingles. Four cargo doors lined the basement wall and the east side, windows above, several of which had been bricked up and painted over in a darker green. The southeast end had a metal overhead door and a man door alongside. An electric light fixture at the peak advertised it as atypical Royale construction. I asked Mick if we could go inside.

There were no locks and she led me into the slightly dank gloom. The light switches didn't turn on any lights, but enough day came through the windows to make out crates of canned goods, sacks of rice and dried beans piled on wooden pallets. Several pieces of equipment lined the opposite wall – three green and yellow utility vehicles parked side by side, their 15-inch tire tracks crisscrossing the dirt floor. Hand tools lay scattered in some of the beds, coiled rope, and each carried a red plastic 5-gallon gas can. I tapped one, found it half full, then crouched to inspect a red and black electric pallet jack, its cowling off, the 24-volt battery terminals corroded. The machine's battery discharge indicator was blank. Machinery struck me as very out of place on the island. I gave Mick a questioning look.

"The men without hearts use these things when their ship comes." She shrugged. "They make much noise in the forest. We hide from them then."

I sat back on my heels, eyeing the inoperative light fixtures hanging from the ceiling. A breaker box on the wall by the man door probably hooked up to an electrical source on the ship to run the lights and recharge the pallet jack. I rose and wandered some more. Unmarked wooden crates along the near wall held folded pants and shirts, the simple designs in black or brown. I rifled through them… three sizes, small, medium, large. One of the crates held underwear, a boy shorts style, all black that looked to be basic cotton. Still another contained plain black canvas slip-on shoes like Mick wore, and another held dark blue woolen hooded cloaks and wool blankets in grey and brown. Farther down, large rectangular olive-drab tins of survival crackers and #10 cans of peanut butter sat stacked in one corner gathering dust. I examined the old, out-dated Civil Defense logo on the boxes, asked Mick if she knew what it meant.

"Uh, uh." She shook her head. "The men without hearts bring all of this when they come on their boat." The peanut butter didn't look as though it had been touched since it was delivered. Mick demurred that no one on the island liked the stuff very much. The canned vegetables were popular, though – corn, green beans, peas and carrots, that sort of thing in generic label #303 or #8Z short cans. Someone had taken some of the tinned meats, too. A careless tumble of cheap tin pots and pans lay in the dirt below the shelving. At the far end of the structure where it was built into the ground, a dug out section served as a simple root cellar now holding bushel baskets of wrinkled carrots, squash, what I thought were parsnips, and something else going to rot that I couldn't immediately identify. It wasn't haute cuisine, but all in all it looked as though someone wanted the Royales to survive and saw to their basic provisions. I filed that away with my growing list of evidence of something. I hadn't concluded exactly what yet. On the way out I grabbed some candles and friction matches from a half-emptied box, shoved them in one of my cargo pockets.

Other days we swam in Duncan Bay, Tobin Harbor, or the waters of Lake Superior itself, surprisingly cold for the time of year. Mick allowed as the current water temperature was about as warm as it ever got. Afterward we'd sit and talk, oddly untroubled by the island's insect life. They were there, black flies, squadrons of mosquitoes, gnats, but for some reason they avoided us. They should have eaten us alive, yet didn't. I couldn't account for it, but didn't complain. Occasionally we camped in the forest or near the lake shore with a small fire and just a couple wool blankets between us and the stars, but most nights we returned to the cottage and kept our own company by candlelight or nothing but the moon's radiance. Our conversations tended toward the less consequential, which I think we both wanted. Our secrets stayed safe with one another that way. I liked those nights best.

The Royales tended to live apart in similar simple cottages and bungalows made of rough logs, or field-stone in some cases, scattered throughout the forest. One day we happened upon what came close to an actual town. We'd hiked Greenstone Ridge to the remote northeastern tip of the island and passed the better part of the afternoon perched on large, rugged boulders there. Gulls circled and a great blue heron picked its way along close to the shore, the lake stretched out beyond him, smooth and peaceful. We ate rice balls that Mick had made, talked and laughed. When the sun sank turning high, thin clouds to fiery orange streaks, it was as if a giant had dragged his paintbrush overhead, giving me an altogether new appreciation for the picturesque. The sun dropped lower extending bright, sparkling fingers across the water toward some far off invisible shore. Plum-colored twilight edged in from the east, slowly lengthening shadows pouring evening into the quiet hollows and bringing us slowly to our feet. Reluctantly, we took our leave.

Mick and I walked hand in hand down a secondary trail and happened upon the place, a collection of houses not so much a community as homes coincidentally located in the same general area. If it had a name, Mick didn't mention it. We followed a central path winding through balsam fir and white spruce, passing silent, shuttered bungalows in the typical saddle-notched and chinked log style, until we came to a clearing. O'Connor lounged under a birch, a thick blade of blue-green grass between his teeth.

"Lad." He gave me a toothy grin. "And ye'r lass. How are ye this evening?"

"Doing okay." I looked around. "Seen Dave?"

"Not for a few days. He may be on the Lady or like as not with another lady. He's spending a fair bit of time down around the Siskiwit. Sena's from by the big river, see." He gave a lazy look around. "Shan's about somewhere."

The place looked deserted, but then the Royales are a retiring lot. Kind of secretive, even. As I had that thought the back of my neck prickled. I couldn't see a soul but felt eyes on us nevertheless. On me. I didn't mention my eerie feeling to O'Connor, but did ask him if he'd given any thought to heading back to the M.

"Not a lick." He smiled broadly. "Not a single lick."

We said good-bye and hiked off through the still hamlet. I cast several glances over my shoulder, holding Mick's hand a little tighter. "You are correct," she murmured, "Someone is watching us."

"The Sovereignty's never going to lift the quarantine on you, you know that?"

"I know that quite well." She sounded more perturbed by our surveillance than the hopelessness of delivery from enforced segregation. She stopped and faced me, taking both my hands. "You understand there are those who look upon me with disfavor?"

"Because you sang to me."

She studied me for a moment, something I couldn't decipher behind those soft brown eyes, then said quietly, "There are other reasons, too, Kim Murayama."

Before she could elaborate a rustle from behind brought me around, reflexively blading the four young men who emerged from the undergrowth. They were perhaps twenty-two years old, twenty-four – somewhere around Mick's age, dressed uniformly in the ubiquitous loose black. Two had brown hair, one black, and the last golden blonde with the yellow cat-eyes lit by angry fire. They fanned out in a semi-circle, blocking our return to town. I'd seen them before – the boys from dinner our first night, the sullen ones whom

Emma didn't know why they were pissed off. Mick slipped out from behind me. "Leave us!" she hissed. "This is not your place, Innis."

"This is not *his* place," the blonde one growled. He gestured sharply at me with a stick, a stout length of finished wood. "Let your great city man be gone."

"He is our guest," Mick grated. Her fists balled.

"Your guest," Innis sneered. "For *your* bed. You who prefers outsiders." His nostrils flared above a cruel smile. "Do not tell us! We are not bewitched of you. We have drunk the wine from our shoes and your enchantment is quitted. A toad laid in sheepskin flayed. I piss in *your* shoe, whore."

Mick started to say more, but I put a hand on her arm. I'd heard enough of this guy's insulting garbage mouth. "Let's see if he knows how to use that thing."

"I will show you how, city man," Innis spat. He gripped the staff in the two-hand low ready position, eyes burning like a pair of hateful suns. He snapped the staff into attack position, extended end no more than six inches from my face. He was probably good, but he was too close, a mistake of inexperience. I grabbed the staff, throwing my right shoulder back as I did and using hip torque to yank the stick toward me. It pulled my opponent off balance. He instantly tried to compensate, pulling back on the staff. I let him, having twisted the opposite end to target his middle. I threw my right shoulder forward now, adding to the momentum and jamming the opposite end of the stick solidly into his lower abdomen. Innis doubled with a painful grunt of surprise, fingers clenching reflexively, but I yanked back, relieving him of his stick altogether. It was a hair under four feet in length, almost identical to the traditional Japanese jo, but lighter. I spun it rapidly, describing a quick Figure 8 in front of me, whipped it vertically down and around behind my right side, then snapped it into a loaded ready position, extended end low with the opposite end resting along my bicep. Pure flash, but it was my intention to advertise.

"Walk away, men," I told them quietly.

Innis surged up, clutching his middle. I snapped the extended end of the staff up, stopping beneath his chin just short of hitting him. Not that he and I would be having tea together, but I *was* a guest, after all. I didn't want to mix it up with the host too much.

"Coward!" Innis sneered. The guy just didn't quit. He needed a lesson in manners. He needed the shit beat out of him.

"You would beat him half to death before he began to understand," Mick murmured.

Innis shot her a vicious look and spat, "A stone to close your opening!"

"Begone!" Mick moved like lightning, her palm cracking across the young man's face before he ever saw it coming. He reeled, hand to his cheek, surprise and shame replacing the anger in his yellow eyes. "Begone, Innis, while you yet may."

Breathing hard, Innis stumbled away toward town, still holding his face. His companions followed with several backward glances. I lowered the staff. With a dispirited sigh Mick sank down where she was, sitting cross-legged in the middle of the path. She propped her chin in her hands and stared glumly. "I apologize. They are a disgrace."

I leaned on the staff. "Is O'Connor gonna' have trouble with them? Maybe we ought to go back."

"They will cause no more trouble now. They have shamed themselves and will be restrained. Another time, however..." She squinted at me and shaded her eyes against the evening sunlight filtering through the branches. "Beware Innis. He is consumed. The others are not so envious, but he leads them where they should not follow."

I crouched beside her. "What did he mean about drinking wine out of shoes?"

Mick shook her head morosely. "It is said to break a spell of enchantment." After a moment she added, "He curses me to be childless as well."

"Why should he do that?"

"Jealousy. He cannot be a father. None of them can. Innis is capable, but naught comes of the act. Devin, Kyle, Boyce... the ones with him. It is the same with all the young men." Sterility, then. Maybe that was why they were so disgruntled. "I have not had sex with Innis or any of his friends, you understand," Mick added.

I shook my head with a wry grin. "That'd be your own business."

"Of course. I only mention it because I have no direct evidence that Innis cannot father children, but the truth of the matter is as I have said." She regarded me intently for a moment, some secret on her lips, then uncoiled and rose in one fluid motion, taking my hand as she stood. "I want to show you something, Kim Murayama."

Mick led me deeper into the forest, pulling me along with a subtle urgency. Shadows grew longer, stalking us along the path. We stopped around a bend and she once again took both my hands. Her eyes glittered, anxious and imperative with the barest hint of malevolence, tempered yet nonetheless dark. I started to step back, but that look froze me. The forest had dimmed with the retreat of day and now it grew blacker. Then everything turned a light, hazy grey and I floated, cushioned by the softness of gently swirling cotton fog, the sensation one of being carried along on an unseen current. I couldn't see Mick, but I felt her grip on my hands and sensed that she wouldn't leave me. Before long the fog lifted, curling, evaporating, and we stood alone on a forested path. The sun still settled, but now through a different line of trees, mountain ash interspersed among spruce and fir. I took quick stock of myself and despite a certainty otherwise found nothing amiss. A polite clearing of the throat got my attention; Mick studied me intently. I gaped in amazement. "What in the hell was *that*?"

"There are paths other than those through the forest. This is Hatchet Lake. Below the Minong." She paused, expression going distant. After a moment she shook herself and pulled me after her, towing me down a narrow path curving through aspen and paper birch. I had no chance to demand a better explanation of how we'd gotten here before we emerged into a clearing holding the tumbled remains of a simple, small bungalow in the Royale style. The roof had fallen in and three of the walls collapsed, the remaining wall charred with blackened timbers leaning from a crumbled stone foundation. Vines and other undergrowth claimed the structure inside and out while raspberry bushes grew wild about the surrounding grounds. I arched a questioning eyebrow at Mick.

"I lived here," she said. "With my mother. The dealers in souls came." Her grip tightened on my hand and she moved closer, her voice almost inaudible. "It was long ago. I was not here. I had gone to Desor, to school by the lake. My mother..." She drew a ragged little breath, but said no more.

I looked over the ruins. There had been a fire, long ago. I disengaged gently from her hand. Mick let me go without comment and I waded carefully through tangled raspberry bushes to the back of the house where she had played or run through the field now choked with brambles and matted, dead grass. The day waned further, one long shadow cast by a single remaining upright timber lengthening slowly toward the thick forest like some forbidding finger pointing east, showing me the way back from where I'd come. For a brief moment, alone there behind the house, I could have sworn the wind was trying to tell me something, too.

Run... It slipped in and out of the trees, whispering around lofty pine tops. *Fly.*

In the thin, fading light I squinted into the dimness of the forest maze beyond, searching for the phantoms so eager that I abandon my search. The wind blew harder, bending the treetops, but whoever or whatever was there didn't show themselves. I continued my walk around, eyeing the ragged field-stone foundation. Within the rubble I saw a broken table, soot-blackened slivers of glass beneath weathered and partially burned cedar shake, silent witnesses to a long ago calamity. How many summers had the ashes been cold? How many snowfalls draped their silent white shroud over this in a vain attempt to soften indelible memory? All was gone now. I could feel the emptiness of Nothing. But even nothing is something.

As I finished my circuitous inspection Mick sat on the remnants of the front steps, knees drawn up under her chin and looking strangely at home. I eased down beside her. The wind snatched at a loose strand of her hair with invisible cold fingers. She ignored it. "What do you find, Kim?"

A little bit of the past, I thought. And some of the future before it was lost. Before it was stolen. I didn't actually see this, but as the great swordsman Musashi says: By knowing that which does not exist, we can know that which does. I looked past her to the pine tops swaying in the ominous wind. "The island's not really safe, is it, Mick?"

"No. It is not. Not now, not ever." She looked over her shoulder at the ruins. "My mother was killed. Here. In our home."

Small, scattered stones outlined the remains of the walkway leading to where we sat. I selected one, rolled it between my fingers, trying to think of something to say. "What about the rest of your family?"

"There was only my mother and me." Mick smiled wistfully.

"Your father..." I ventured, though I thought I already knew the answer.

"I do not have a father." Her expression hardened. "But I am a real person, Kim. I am in here." She pressed one small fist between her breasts. "Not Emma or Sena or Shanna or even Edrea. Only me. I smile when I am happy and I cry when I am sad. And when the Darkness comes I am afraid. I am alone then. In here." Her fist remained balled to her chest. "You made us, but we are not what you expected. You do not want us, yet you must have us. We are compelled to stay on the island, but you steal us away. Why do you think Emma looks so much like Miriam, and she like me? Why I have no father. You are not a foolish man, Kim Murayama. Surely you suspect the truth of matters." It couldn't be, but... "Say it."

"All right. You're a clone, aren't you?"

She nodded tightly, jaw clenched with the confession, if that's what it was. I sat back and lifted my eyes to dark clouds. No wonder Doc Fredericks didn't want me digging up trouble. The IPO may not have done well, but the process worked. God blessed never die immortality. "Here is not like your great city. Not at all." Mick sighed despondently. "I am not like you. If you no longer want me, I understand."

She wasn't like *any* woman I'd ever met. I didn't know exactly what she was, but I knew she was real and I was pretty sure she was what I wanted, contraband or no. "That's not the case, Mick."

She sighed with understated relief, but nibbled her lower lip. "Perhaps I go farther than is prudent."

"Perhaps we both do."

She studied me intently for several seconds, then said, "You told me of Joanna. I understand now. At least a little. Do you wish to understand more of me?"

I looked at the ruined house, then at Mick. I nodded wordlessly.

She shifted to face me. "Let me touch you." Her fingertips rested lightly on my temples, her gaze suddenly hypnotic and inescapable. For a frozen moment we sat like that in front of the ruined bungalow.

Then it began.

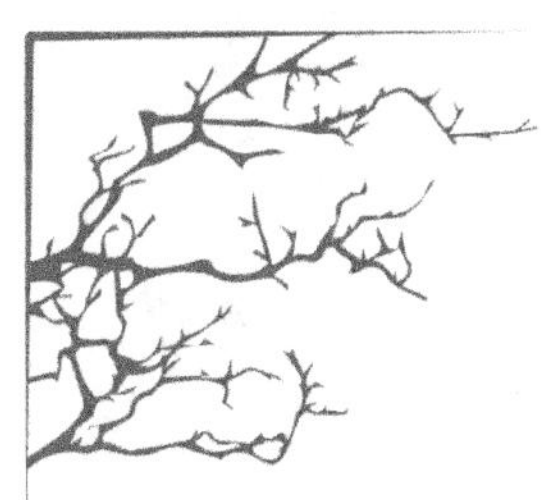

Chapter 10

Hazy figures bend over a table, their words unclear in antiseptic air and the whisper of mechanical breathing. A face turns toward me, dark, unfeeling eyes above a surgical blue mask. It stares, then straightens holding a small, blood-smeared bundle. Tiny arms and legs struggle helplessly as it's carried away beyond an opaque curtain while a weak voice pleads from the table.

She is perhaps 18 years old, maybe younger. Blood soaks the sheets beneath her. Perspiration trickles down her neck and face, brown hair sweat-matted and tangled. It isn't Mick, but it could be. The figures ignore her, concerned only with stainless steel and catheters. She calls upon her sisters, implores them, cries out for her mother. Her pleas fall on ears that do not hear, on hearts that do not feel. My fists clench, but just when it seems the tearful entreaties will never cease they dwindle to a single curious voice.

"Mother?"

A songbird trills beneath blue skies and boughs rustle gently, but my nose wrinkles at the smell of burned wood and scorched earth. A little girl with large brown eyes stands at the edge of the pines. I follow her gaze to the smoldering remains, the fire barely burned out. Charred timbers lie jumbled upon the collapsed foundation; grey ash swirls as bitter smoke twists skyward. Blackened hands, flesh seared and curling, reach hopelessly from the past. The little girl with large brown eyes comes to me and her fingertips touch my temples.

Then flames explode, a nightmare within a nightmare. Oil lamps flare and sconces shatter, glass crunching beneath heavy boots. My stomach lurches, overwhelmed by the stench of kerosene mixed with pine, sweat and fear. With cinnamon and hate.

Wood splinters. Hulking shapes move through flashes in the darkness. A woman is thrust roughly to the floor, her hair disheveled, tangled across terror-filled brown eyes in an oval face. Shards of glass slice her palms, her slim, tapered fingers. The coppery tang of fresh blood mixes with the reek of petroleum.

Black, greasy smoke billows and fire springs to life. It races up the walls, laps at the ceiling and bounds across the floor, a frenzied creature scenting the kill. Its breath roars, a storm sucking great droughts of air as it charges. The beast upon her! Screams pierce my ears. I grab her wrist, but blackened skin sloughs off with the sound of sizzling bacon. She's on fire. Her hair, her clothing, everything on fire. I'm on fire- I'm burning!

"No! No, you are not!" Hands seize me. "It is over." Mick gripped my arms, face close. "Come back, Kim. Come back."

Heart hammering, I inhaled great lungfuls of delicious fresh air. Perspiration dripped from my eyebrows, the tip of my nose. "Jesus Christ…"

"You are safe," she whispered, breath wonderfully cool on my cheek. "All is well now. I only showed you what was. It is no longer real."

"Your-" I swallowed, tried again. "Your mother."

"Her name was Theresa."

The little girl. "Was that you? Was the little girl you?"

"It was me. It was Emma and Miriam. She is all of us." All the Royales in a witch world of fire and pain. Of fear. "Now you know. The past is your memory as well."

Yes, I knew. And I wished to God I didn't.

Mick regarded me for a moment, then sat back. "My mother was of the Light. She challenged the fear that haunts the forests and lives in the darkness, here on the island. But in your world, too, Kim Murayama." She put her hand gently on my chest. "In your hearts." I started to reply, then didn't. She didn't mean me personally. "No, I do not mean you," she went on, "Your world is vast and strange. It changes us and kills us. The Darkness lives there as well. The eyes you felt before? On the beach and in the wood. They see for those who prey on us all."

The little stone lay on the ground between my feet. I must have dropped it. I wondered if it had been there when the fire burned. I squinted at Mick, wondering What if the dealers in souls didn't come any more?

"We need a champion," she whispered. "I need one."

That was when I determined to be that for her. To hell with the psychology of it. I wouldn't be too late the hero this time. "I'll have to find Dave"

Mick stood. "Come with me." She drew me to my feet. Tendrils of foggy grey wound about us again and we drifted, holding hands.

FULL NIGHT PRESSED down like the ocean depths as we arrived back at the cottage. Black clouds streamed overhead, a menacing river of evil overflowing the banks of the sky. Pines bent under the wind's roar as it howled through the treetops. Mick staggered, pummeled by the vicious gusts. "Kim!" she shouted. "It is the Darkness! It knows!"

A bang sounded from behind. Dave stood on the porch, Sena behind him struggling to hold the door open. "Murayama! God damn!" Dave fought his way down the steps against the wind, pulling the tall blonde Royale after him. "We're getting out of here!"

"What the hell's going on?" I yelled. Dust, leaves and sticks whirled madly.

"I don't know! Some kind of witch shit! Let's go!"

I didn't see O'Connor anywhere, but the urge to flee overpowered that concern. My heart raced with inexplicable fear. Beyond the clearing angry black clouds rose, clawing one over another, up and up as the wind shrieked, slashing sharp and cold. We ran for the bay as rain came, stinging daggers of ice. Thunder rumbled, then welled, exploding through the heavens. I ducked involuntarily. Gale force winds cracked limbs all around us. Sena and Dave crashed through the undergrowth, wet branches slapping, cutting the tall blonde's cheek. Lightning burned the air blue-white.

"Shit!" I shielded my eyes and stumbled on until we burst onto the beach; Mick's chest heaved beneath her wet shirt, water running down her face. Farther up, two figures scrambled toward us.

"Liam!" Dave broke from the trees, Sena in tow. The big Irishman's head came up and he redoubled his efforts, running hard. Shanna stumbled behind him, one small hand enveloped in his massive grip. Our little skiff rocked at the water's edge, and beyond, through thick, grey sheets of rain the *Shady Lady* rolled and tossed in violent waters. Dave took off for the skiff, dragging Sena with him, but I stood rooted, staring. A towering column of churning blackness rose above the trees, magic and monstrous, horribly alive. From the peak of the mass slitted, inhuman eyes glared balefully. At me.

"Murayama! Come on!" Dave was at the skiff. Waves crashed over our little boat, deluging him and Sena.

O'Connor reached them, faltered and went to one knee, the murky, churning water striving to drag him under, but he came up snarling. He grabbed onto the skiff even harder and thrust his arm at Shanna, hand open. "Come on, girl!" She recoiled, green eyes wide. I heard her cry.

"I cannot, Liam!"

"Are ye daft! Come on with ye!" She drew back further, holding her head, tears of panic and terror mixing with the pounding rain. Dave reached for her, too, but Sena hauled him up short.

"We cannot go with you!" Mick shouted to me above the tumult. She pushed wet, matted hair from her eyes. "Save yourself. I beg you. I will be all right." She didn't sound as though she believed her own words, but she put both hands on my chest and shoved me hard. "Go! Hurry!"

All three Royales scrambled up the beach toward the trees. I started to follow, but Dave's grip closed on my arm. "What the fuck, Murayama?"

"I don't know what the fuck, Dave!"

"If we're not taking our leave now we'll not be taking it at all!" O'Connor cried, straining to keep the skiff from being torn free. He jabbed a finger at the bay. "See there!"

The *Lady* rolled hard, gunwales dipping perilously. Waves broke over her foredeck. O'Connor was right, in a few minutes we wouldn't be able to go. Dave's fists clenched. He hesitated only a moment, then snarled. "My boat! Let's go, O'Connor! Move!"

O'Connor heaved. The skiff slid into the tumbling waters of Duncan Bay. Dave splashed after it and threw his weight against the pitching boat. I should have jumped in and helped them, should have boarded the *Shady Lady* and sailed away from this unearthly madness. I started to. I waded into the swirling water, but stopped to look back. Sena and Shanna were gone, vanished into the storm-lashed forest. Mick lagged behind, though. She went down on hands and knees short of the tree line. She struggled erect and turned toward me, drenched and swaying. Our eyes met through the driving rain and I knew she'd been wrong. She would not be all right.

Yeah, I should have gone home, but I went the other way. It might as well have been Joanna in the alley.

I charged through the howling gale, reaching her as she collapsed. I dropped to my knees, quickly checking the woods for the other two. They weren't there, but something else was. I saw it. I saw the Darkness face to face. It came to earth, a great rolling black mass from a lowering sky, filling the forest and racing over the ground. It rumbled through the trees, billowing round them. The wind hammered at me, cold and stinking like the draft from a slaughterhouse. My stomach lurched, trying to empty itself. More than ever I wanted to run, to get as far away from this unspeakable horror as I could. I almost broke, almost left Mick lying there, Dave and O'Connor to face whatever fate waited. The Darkness could have them. It could have them, the *Lady*, and all the M.

But I didn't run. The first ghastly tendrils, poisonous and inky, slithered from the woods to lick at Mick's feet. I slapped at them, then sprang into a middle stance.

"You can't fight it that way!" Dave was beside me, reaching for her. "Get her other arm!"

I did as he said and we dragged Mick unceremoniously to the water's edge. O'Connor had the skiff's motor running and tilled us through battering surf. Water exploded over the gunwales; I wrapped my arms around Mick's limp body trying to shield her from the worst of it. Awash, half submerged, we reached the *Lady*. O'Connor brought us alongside and Dave leaped aboard. "Never mind the skiff!" he shouted. The big Irishman didn't hesitate. He sprang forward, helping me wrestle Mick to her feet and heaving her up. O'Connor boosted me and followed, then charged off behind Dave. I rolled over, gasping, saw the skiff slide from sight, swallowed by the roiling bay. Across the churning surface the Darkness pursued. The *Lady*'s engines ground to life as I grabbed Mick's collar and dragged her toward the hatch. Choking blackness closed in, but I concentrated on getting her below to her cabin.

Somehow we made it out of Duncan Bay through the narrow channel and into open water. The *Lady* heeled dangerously, but Dave fought the wheel and held her true. I crawled to the porthole. Lightning pulsed angrily inside immense thunderheads, furious yet falling behind as though restricted to that strange, alien place. I sank down, back pressed to the bulkhead, and hung my head between my knees, trying to catch my breath.

Mick curled in a ball on the bunk, shivering uncontrollably, black shirt and pants molded to her. I climbed to my feet and found two wool blankets stowed in the cabin's small closet. I set them aside for the moment and pulled her saturated clothing off. I had her bundled in the blankets when Dave stepped in, dripping on the deck, a towel clenched in one fist.

"She okay?" He scowled, but his eyes held a haunted look.

"I think so." I finished tucking the blankets around Mick and stood. "We clear?"

"Yeah." Dave leaned against the door frame and ran a hand down his face. Water beaded his brushcut stubble. His jaw worked for a moment, then, "What the Christ you doing? You shouldn't have brought her along."

"I couldn't leave her, Dave." Like I'd left Jo. He had to know that. But for all we'd accomplished we could have just as well stayed in the M and saved ourselves a whole lot of time, money, and grief. We were back where we'd started. Worse, even.

"This is what I've been trying to get through your stupid head," Dave growled. "Things ain't like they were. I'm trying to make a living. I can't have you blowing in with shitloads of trouble, then blowing out leaving me holding the bag. We ain't kids no more." He wiped his face with the towel. "Jesus Christ. Save the world, why don't you?"

I wasn't trying to save the world. If I had been I'd have been home to save Jo. I think that's what Dave meant. I thought he resented that Sena didn't come with us, too. Mick said they couldn't, yet here she was. I looked up at him and said flatly, "You didn't have to wait."

"Yes, I did. I couldn't leave you, Murayama. Sometimes I wish I could, but I never can." I understood. There had been times in the Reserves – Stillwater, with the bodies of the Samaritans strewn about the street and the field beyond town or the fight on Big Tree Mountain when the Warlord of Harrisburg would have slaughtered us all. The Piedmont and half a dozen other places you've never heard of. I didn't leave him and he didn't leave me. He glared for a few more seconds, then flung the towel at me with a spray of water and a muttered, "Fuck. Get yourself dried off" before turning and clumping away.

I sat on the edge of the bunk and rubbed Mick's back through thick wool. Someone – or something – was definitely pissed off at us. Maybe for spending time with the locals, but I thought it more than simple, frivolous dalliance that angered the sky. Mick was only the tip of the iceberg. I'd seen storms before, even rode out a vicious one on Lake Ontario with Dave and O'Connor one time, but I'd never seen anything like what had just come after us at Duncan Bay. I'd never been so scared in my life, a visceral, incomprehensible fear that only now, miles away, didn't make me want to throw up. Still wet and a little cold, I shifted, cradling Mick. She burrowed close, snuggling deep in the wool, her breathing slow and barely audible. Before long her body heat warmed me enough that my eyelids began to droop. I put my head back, held the Royale, and listened to the *Lady* creak as we drove through the deep Lake Superior night.

I dozed fitfully until a thin, watery dawn seeped past the porthole glass. Grey clouds hung low, reluctant to give the new day much room. Mick stirred in her wool cocoon, blinked sleepily at me, then sat bolt upright with a violent start. "Kim!"

I smiled. "Good morning."

She exhaled a shaky breath and leaned against me, eyes closing again. "You came back for me," she whispered. "You should not have."

I didn't consider her ungrateful. Mick was too ingenuous to intentionally bruise my ego and, frankly, it might be worse for her back in the M, though with the storm still fresh in my mind and my heart rate barely returned to normal I somehow doubted that. It was far more than a rainstorm.

"It was the Darkness," Mick said in a tremulous whisper. She called it Night itself, an angry rush down paths other than those through the forest, the gift of speaking without speaking bellowing in mindless rage. It was the knowing of another heart and breaking it. She made it sound alive, that if we'd stayed it would've devoured us. And because I couldn't leave her to that, she was going back to the M that wanted her dead just as badly. Mick snuffled softly. "For me it no longer matters. My destiny is prescribed. I have told you, Kim Murayama. I shall not live half so long as you."

I held her for a while longer, then got up to hang our clothes to dry, see if Dave had anything stuffed away in the cabin's locker for the meantime.

WE DROPPED ANCHOR ON the western side of Goulais Bay not far north of Sault Ste. Marie. I wasn't familiar with Goulais Mission at all – never knew the place existed, frankly – but Dave contended that the Ojibways of Goulais Mission 15A would likely be interested in buying a few greenstones and completely indifferent as to Canadian Customs being any the wiser. Mick and I lounged at the port rail watching him and O'Connor row toward a leaning dock too small to accommodate the *Shady Lady*, but hosting a couple of runabouts, one stern-drive, the other outboard, and a homegrown houseboat constructed of plywood walls and a canvas roof, all affixed atop dented pontoons that so far had kept it all afloat. From the porch of Nobby's General Store a trio of locals watched, too, from under a mix of hand-painted and stamped tin signs advertising bait, tackle, cold beer, groceries and guns. There were some houses farther up a dirt road past the store, fixer-uppers that hadn't been yet, an RV on blocks. It didn't strike me as the Canadian diamond district, but Dave was adamant. He'd put in here before, he said, knew his business and I should mind my own. He was right on all three counts.

"Twenty-three Bobby's for one." Dave held up a wad of Canadian bank notes. "And thirty big Bobs for the other." All in the brown-tinged polymer Canadian hundred dollar denomination that would be worth close to ten thousand in Sovereignty Bs at the current exchange rate. He peeled off one bill, thrust it at me. I turned it over, not recognizing the image I supposed to be Bobby Whomever on the obverse, more intrigued with the reverse showing a DNA double-helix and a vial of something. As I considered what this might augur, if it augured anything at all, Dave snatched the bill from my fingers. "Fifty-three hundred. I just wanted you to see it so you know I was right and you were wrong." He slapped O'Connor on the back. "We're shitting in high cotton, Liam. *High* cotton!"

Mick tugged at my sleeve. "Why did you not accept greenstones from Edrea? She would have given them."

I nodded slowly to myself. I bet she would have.

Late in the day we paid to transit the Soo Locks with some of the money from Goulais and headed up the St. Mary's River. Rather than risk passage into to Lake Huron after dark we dropped anchor for the night in the north end of Lake George off Echo Bay. I think Dave could have negotiated the way south, but I guessed he wanted to relax a little. I could hear him and O'Connor laughing and drinking on the flying bridge. I didn't join them, instead leaning on the stern rail contemplating the scattered lights of what appeared a vastly rural area along the north shore, wondering how I got here, where I'd come from and, more importantly, where I was headed. No epiphany manifested and after a time, with no clear insight, I went below. I cracked the door to Mick's cabin. Her bunk was empty, but I needn't have worried. I found her in mine.

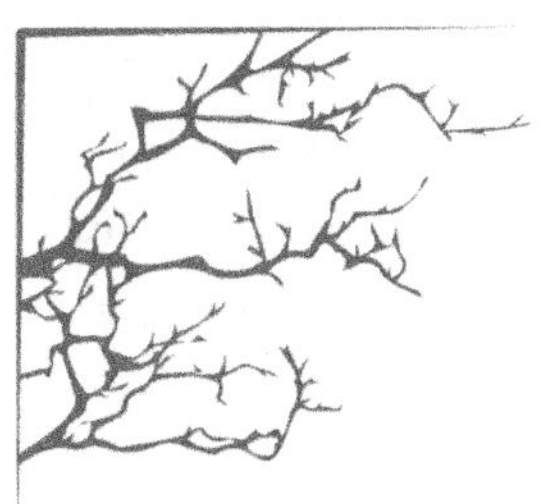

Chapter 11

We passed through the Mississagi Strait between Cockburn Island and the much larger Manitoulin Island not long after sunrise the next morning. Dave swung the *Lady* wide to the southeast, but stayed well away from the international border cutting Lake Huron down its center. Once in the clear he turned her due south for the long haul to Sarnia and the entrance to the St. Clair River. He kept the throttle open and by 7:00 the next morning O'Connor picked up Goderich marine band on the radio. "Sarnia by noon," he said.

Dave allowed that he'd be going ashore there to unload some more greenstones before we were back in the Sovereignty. Customs could be trouble; this wasn't an Ojibway reserve, but I didn't argue. Emeralds would be an even bigger problem in the Sovereignty.

We put in just before noon, the *Lady* easing slowly up to the dock behind a lake freighter loading petrochemical product from the forest of smokestacks sprouting as far as the eye could see. While O'Connor tossed lines ashore and got us tied up, Dave cut the engines and turned to me. "Watch the boat. And hide the witch. This ain't gonna' be like Goulais."

Where do you hide a witch, huh? I told him okay and went looking for Mick. I found her in the galley, staring out a porthole. "Dave's worried about Customs," I told her.

Mick cocked her head. "Mores, yes?" She pronounced it *mor-ayz* in the correct manner so seldom encountered. "The proper conventions to be observed in these circumstances." She didn't get the full import. Isle Royale doesn't have police. They have the Darkness instead. I cleared my throat. "They're going to look on the Lady and if they find you... I don't know what Canada might do with an illegal, but it probably won't be good, Mick." I made a small empty gesture with one hand. "We ought to hide you somewhere."

"They will not find me." She flashed a quick, reassuring grin and slipped across the deck, feet silent in soft black shoes. She stood on tiptoe and gave me a feathery kiss on the cheek and whispered earnestly, "Trust me, Kim Murayama."

With everything at stake and no real basis for it, I did. And they didn't find her. They looked, but they didn't find her.

As soon as we docked Customs came aboard all uniformed and official. Polite and civil, but all business. Dave accompanied them as they looked everywhere. O'Connor leaned against the rail amidships, arms folded across his broad chest. "They're looking for something in particular," he opined.

I nodded absently. There was no sign of Mick. None. For all that had happened I could have dreamed her.

You do not dream me, Kim Murayama. Someone gave my hand a ghostly squeeze.

I started, but forced myself to relax. O'Connor noticed nothing. I leaned back against the rail, careful not to look at what wasn't there as Dave stalked up accompanied by an officer and two ratings. He pointed at us. "That's O'Connor and that's Murayama. My crew."

The one with gold braid sized us up, then to Dave, "This boat went to Duluth."

"Grand Marais, actually," Dave replied. "Below Thunder Bay. 'Bout a third of the way down the coast."

"I know where it is. Quite a storm up that way a day or two ago. Below Thunder Bay."

Dave shrugged. "Must have missed it."

"You weren't in the vicinity of Isle Royale, then?"

"Hell, no. That's posted."

"Indeed." The inspector flipped through some papers. "You list nothing on your manifest."

"We were gonna' buy, but nobody was selling."

"Not a very profitable trip, Captain Hanson."

"No," Dave agreed amicably, "it wasn't." Whether they believed that or not, Customs departed as satisfied as they were likely to get. Dave ordered O'Connor to get a move on. "We got emeralds to sell." Personally, I thought he was pushing the envelope a little hard, but all my opinion got was, "They don't know shit. I told you this trip would be a lot of trouble and by Jesus I'm going to be compensated- Liam! God damn. Let's go!"

As they thumped down the gangplank the air next to me murmured, "Mr. Hanson is still upset."

Again I managed not to jump. Then, out the side of my mouth, I hissed, "What the fuck are you doing?" I fumbled until I got hold of a hand I couldn't see, then pulled her through the hatch and down to the galley. When I turned around she was there again. "You turned invisible!"

She slid onto the bench at the table, staring at a single apple on a dented tin plate and refusing to look at me. "I was not exactly invisible."

"What were you then, exactly?"

She stared at the fruit as though the answer might somehow be found in the shiny red skin. "To be invisible is to be unable to be seen. To disappear is to become lost to sight. If I were invisible, no one could see me. Because I disappeared does not mean those men could not see me. They simply did not." She finally looked up at me, her expression mostly apologetic. "They did not look."

"I looked. I didn't see you either."

"You could have." She gave me a contrite smile. "If you looked hard enough." After a moment she added, "You see things that others do not."

Eyes like tekagi – See Beyond. Shiyro had taught me, but at the moment I didn't feel very perceptive. I didn't see how she could do that. The woman turned invisible. Disappeared. "I want to know how you did that."

"I told you."

"All due respect, Mick, but you told me shit."

She scowled. "Your language is atrocious." That had been advanced before; the caliber of my speech certainly didn't measure up anywhere near her Victorian articulation. And if a profane word ever passed her lips it wasn't when I'd been within earshot.

I chuckled ruefully and went to get some coffee. "Okay. Don't tell me." Everybody has their secrets, but I judged this surely another reason she was quarantined. People are afraid of what they don't understand. I wondered if she could stay invisible forever, which was about how long she'd need to if the Sovereignty decided to dissect her and find out how that worked.

"It would profit them not at all!" she snarled.

She was doing it again. My coffee cup banged on the counter, slopping java, and I rounded on her, unsure whether my temper was provoked by this incessant thought stealing or simply exasperation with her naivety. Or both. "They'd do it anyhow. They want your DNA. They want to live forever. And if they can learn to read minds or disappear by cutting your head open and pawing through your brain pan, they will. They'll carve you up and throw away what's left when they're finished. God damn it, lady, this is the M we're talking about."

She looked away. "I know."

Not really she didn't. If she truly understood she'd jump screaming overboard. Better to drown than suffer the God damned M. Maybe she couldn't see everything in my head after all. I drank some coffee that had stayed in the cup and let things settle. Mick stared unseeing at the apple in front of her. At length I said, "We'll go back to Doc Fredericks'. I think he might know how we can find your friends. The dealers in souls."

"They are not my friends," Mick replied thinly. "I know that much about your M."

WE MADE LAKE ST. CLAIR late in the afternoon. The smoke from Dead Detroit was worse than ever, but Dave didn't seem to mind. Three more greenstones sold in Sarnia and another 3400 Bobbys in his pocket probably helped his attitude. He took the *Lady* through the lake and down the river whistling all the way. The pall and stench fell behind as we cleared Windsor on the Canadian side, then ran between Amherstburg and Colchester while again scrubbing the *Lady*'s decks down. She was pretty well cleaned when we passed between Point Pelee and Pelee Island. The setting sun decorated Lake Erie's surface, orange and purple fingers gently drawing the night over us from beyond the horizon. We had some supper in the galley with O'Connor, beans and canned peaches. Mick passed on the beans, eating in silence, and excused herself quickly. Dave came down when O'Connor relieved him at the helm. I did up the dishes and we had a cup of coffee together, Dave making sure I understood the game plan. "Once we're in the M, get the witch off my boat,"

he said. "You want a contraband around your neck, that's your business, but she ain't gonna' sink *my* boat. You copy?"

"Copy that, Dave." I couldn't blame him. I had no idea what I was getting into, not even a real plan of what I was going to do. I finished putting away the dishes and went to my cabin which, not so much to my surprise, but to my disappointment, was empty. I didn't turn on a light, just lay on the bunk, staring at the overhead, wondering if there was any hope for Mick in the M and, selfishly and probably wholly unrealistically, if there might be any for me and her. I knew in my heart that such hopes were no more than dark, empty nights. I was trying not to review my lengthy list of barren hopes that forces itself to the surface for review at times like this when a hesitant knock interrupted my maundering. "Yeah."

The door cracked open just enough to admit Mick's head and one shoulder from the shadowed passageway. Her voice came soft and uncertain. "Kim? May I come in? I do not want to be alone."

Neither did I. I held out a hand. She slipped in and closed the door quietly, then padded over and crawled onto the bunk with me. I put an arm around her; she pressed close, silent in the gloom and more than I had hoped for of a dark, hollow night. Neither of us spoke and eventually I slept, dreamless, but waking with a vague, lingering sense of dread that evaporated only slowly with the first light of dawn. Mick lay on her side watching me without expression. "Are you afraid of me now?" she whispered.

"No." Just mystified. And what woman isn't mystifying, eh? Mick was simply more mystery than most. I kissed her forehead, receiving a relieved smile in return. I gave her a pat on her hip. "Let's see if coffee's on." I still didn't know what I was going to do with her, or with us, but she was here and that was good enough for the moment.

By 8.00 am we approached Port Colborne, making our way into the Welland Canal within the hour. We slid north past the rising grain elevators and a large black lake freighter taking on its cargo of corn or soybeans. The nickel refinery trickled thin white smoke into the morning air. In the early afternoon, approaching the double locks at Thorold, I found Mick gazing at the old cemetery to starboard.

"You put your dead in the ground." Her eyes never left the weathered stones.

"Some people do. What sort of arrangements do you make on the island?"

"The dead are given to the waters." Mick started to say something more, then stopped, lips compressed. Her eyes grew suddenly moist and she turned away. "You remember when the sky was angry? On the lake, when we left your great city before. And what you saw at Duncan Bay."

I'd never forget, but I said, "That's behind us, Mick," implying some future for the two of us that remained unseen and unknowable.

"No," she said wistfully. "The Darkness will never be content but that I am chastened." I feared that I understood all too well. We might dally, she and I, but I was Outside. Dangerous, to be kept without. And the M, my world, would never have her. It would destroy her. This was what I had brought her back to, condemned to her own destruction. I wanted to tell her she could stay with me – where, how, I had no idea. I only knew that I wanted to be with the mystical witch. Mick turned, putting her palms on my chest, her eyes glittering in the dimness like lightning flashes from a distant summer storm over her faraway island. "Hear me. There are things in my world that you cannot imagine. Wonderful things and terrible things thrust good and bad upon one without choice. They cannot be changed, not by fighting, not by tears. Not even by love. I am in love with you, Kim Murayama, and as I would be with you then do I sentence you to death."

That didn't sound good at all, no, but I didn't care. I loved her, too, as wonderful and terrible as that might be for both of us, and I thought then to say the words. I started to, but couldn't, the pernicious twins Guilt and Self-denial chalking up another goal. Yet, under the early evening stars, in the face of my silence, Mick laid one soft fingertip to my lips and whispered, "If you never speak at all I will know what is in your heart." She knew. Enchanted or bewitched, Mick knew I was in love with her.

I was under her spell.

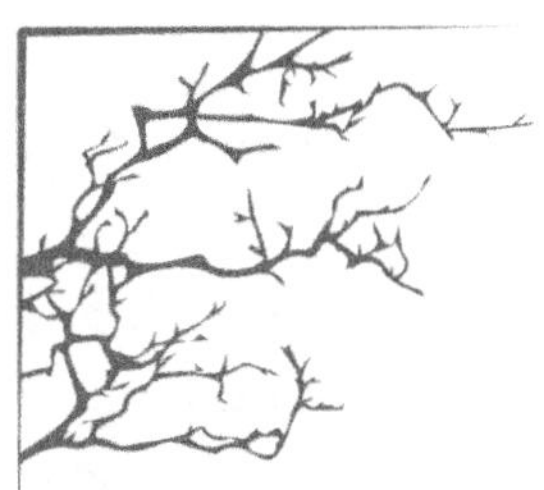

Chapter 12

Before three more days passed we tied up in the M, the *Lady* resting dockside in scummy water and the pervasive stench of rotting fish. O'Connor inhaled deeply. "Ahhh... home."

Sovereignty Customs didn't even grin. They set to tearing things apart – lockers emptied below, galley cupboards dumped, cushions cut open in every cabin. They slashed half a dozen life vests, scattering kapok everywhere. When they found nothing they searched us. There were nine agents in brown uniforms of varying uniformity – short sleeves, long sleeves, a sleeveless once-white undershirt under a black leather cross-belt. They were armed and, with the exception of the sergeant and the man frisking us at the rail, all those guns seemed pointed at me. Dave had hidden the emeralds and the Bobbys well, wherever he'd put them. They found nothing and we were grudgingly declared clean. "Like their boat," the sergeant grunted. He held a truncheon, leather thong tight about his wrist. "Not a God damned thing on the whole boat."

"I told you," Dave said thinly. "Nobody was selling."

"That's not what I hear," the sergeant said. "I hear you got a pretty good haul."

"What big ears you have."

The end of the billy suddenly jammed up under Dave's chin. His head jerked back as the sergeant stepped in close. "Maybe a taste of the wood'll adjust that attitude."

Dave's fists balled. His biceps bulged but he didn't swing. Instead he grated between clenched teeth, "That stick's gonna' be past tense somewhere you don't get it outa' my face."

O'Connor grinned at me and winked. "He means the stick is gonna' be stuck, bub. Up somebody's ass." For a long, frozen moment no one moved. The sergeant's jaw worked as he tried to decide on his next step. It's always foolish to jump froggy like that without a plan as to where you're going with it. Kind of like I was with Mick, but in this instance I'd picked my targets. One man was close enough to disarm, then I could shoot at least two more before they took me out and it didn't matter whether I had a plan for myself and Mick. O'Connor's a big guy, he'd get two more, and I'd seen Dave throw a man before. The sergeant would be overboard before the rest of the fight was hardly started. We'd be high on the Sovereignty's shit list afterward – more trouble I'd have gotten Dave into – but at the moment that wasn't a concern. I kept my expression neutral and held my tongue, gauging my move.

Nose to nose with the sergeant, Dave asked quietly, "Think it's worth it?"

The sergeant apparently grasped the implications, if not the actual dynamics. There was nothing actionable yet – close, but not quite – and by the time there was he wouldn't be around to care one way or the other. He relaxed and gave Dave a manufactured smile. "All right, captain. I guess that's all." The billy shook, but impotently, and the agents slouched away a most vengeful kind of disgruntled. O'Connor watched them go up the quay.

"I'm thinking the secrets of Lake Superior an't quite so secret," the big Irishman mused. "Witches and all."

Dave joined us. "If there isn't one on my boat I got nothing to worry about. Where the Christ did you hide her?"

"I got rid of her," I said. Just like he wanted.

"Well, it's time you and her said good-bye, anyway. It's been a trip, Murayama. If you ever need a boat again, call somebody else."

To hell with it. If I needed to go back up there bad enough I'd walk.

I turned to leave. Dave stopped me at the gangplank. He proffered a wad of Canadian dough. "The witch ought to have some more clothes or something. Some food. If she depends on you she'll be fucking destitute inside of a week."

I took the money with a curt nod and clumped down the gangplank to the dock. The air beside me murmured quietly, "Could you do that? Walk to my island."

I grinned, eyes straight ahead. "Yeah, I could. Dead Detroit'd be a pain in the ass, but I could do it."

"All the way?"

"All the way, Mick." I held out my hand. Spectral fingers closed on mine.

THE THIRD PLATE DAVE had given me worked – some guy named Alfred Abbot. There was no way of knowing how long this scam might last before the authorities flagged him or Herb or Foster Balch, but we got away with it once more. This time I tapped the keypad and told it to charge Alfie two fares, maybe keep the Transit Authority looking for somebody else. We took the Tube to the Chinese Wall and headed for the clinic, winding our way through panhandlers and dealers. A couple of leggy working girls loitered on a corner, tattooed from neck to ankles in multi-hued flowers that marked them as belonging to Greene Issac's stable. They invited me for some inexpensive fun and when I declined they invited Mick. The Royale only moved closer to me and didn't dignify their laughing suggestions with a reply. At the clinic Doc Fredericks stood in the open doorway to his office in his faded white lab coat, staring as though surprised to see us.

"Kim. What are you doing here?" Then, recovering his manners, he invited us in. He didn't sound as if he really wanted to, but he offered us a seat on the old sofa and closed the door. "I thought you were taking her back where she belongs."

I gave him a brief outline of my theory, that the Royales were being abducted off their island for their telomerase. For God blessed never die immortality. Doc took a seat behind his desk, folded his hands on the blotter as though discussing a poor diagnosis that he hated to break to a patient, a light sheen of perspiration glistening on his forehead. "That's pretty far-fetched, Kim."

"Stranger things."

He looked away, out the window as though searching for an escape, fingertips drumming nervously on the desk. "What I told you was medical research." He spread his hands and forced a barely perceptible smile to act like a grin. At the window. "Old research. Speculative. It's abandoned now. Immortality doesn't exist."

"I think they're stealing it off Isle Royale. This month."

His expression grew even more brittle. "You just don't know when to quit, do you?"

I didn't give a shit what he thought. I wanted to know who was doing it and he knew an awful lot about a search for something that didn't exist. "Gimme a name."

Now he looked at me, his uneasiness almost palpable. "What for?"

"Because when I find them they're going to stop what they're doing- Christ, what's wrong with you? You act like you wish you'd never met me."

"That is exactly how he feels," Mick murmured.

The weak smile collapsed altogether. He pointed a trembling finger at Mick. "Get her away from me, Murayama. Get her out of here."

I had to wonder what else she perceived, what truths Doc might be camouflaging with his concocted anger and which he feared the witch would see through. I stood and looked down at him. "Give me some place else to go."

He squeezed his eyes shut and whispered tightly, "You don't want to do this, Kim."

"Oh, but I do."

Now his expression turned suspicious. "Is this noble undertaking your idea? There's every chance this is her crusade, not yours." When my only reply was an unwavering glare, he held his head in his hands. "Wilmut. Wilmut, Incorporated. Across the river." I gave a curt nod, took Mick's hand and walked to the door. We were almost there when Doc cleared his throat. "Murayama. Kim. Wait." He exhaled heavily. "Look, if it turns out you have nowhere else to go... I mean, nowhere at all."

"Sure, Doc. Thanks."

"Don't mention it. To anyone."

Once outside we walked quickly, close to the buildings, as far from the curb as I could get us and eyeballing every doorway and alley as a avenue of attack and potential line of retreat should we be challenged. Nothing I saw suggested we were under surveillance or in danger of being stopped, but Doc's jumpiness was contagious. Mick clung tightly to my hand. "Where are we going, Kim?"

"Jack's." I needed a place to think. And a beer. We crossed the street, sprinting in front of a city bus trailing blue-white diesel exhaust, then cutting off the Strip to get over to Jack's Place. We pushed through his door trading the warm day for cool dimness and anonymity. Under the stamped tin ceiling nondescript figures hunched at the bar drinking their late lunches in the chronic gloom of the place. Jack was behind the stick and waved when we came in. "Hey, Murayama. How you doing?" The forced cordiality was brittle as a twig.

I waved without a word and headed toward the back, ushering Mick between some empty tables. We took a dark corner booth. One of the bar waitresses, Pam, came right away; I ordered a hamburger and a draft. She looked questioningly at Mick. "Maybe some onion soup," I said. I thought Mick might like that. Pam took our order and left us alone in the shadows. I watched Jack surreptitiously watching us as he drew drafts and wiped glasses. Mick sat primly, her palms resting on the table, eyes closed. After a few moments her brow drew down in a puzzled frown. Behind the bar Jack suddenly froze, a glass in one hand, a bottle in the other, his expression a mix of curiosity and mild consternation.

"Thirty pieces of silver," Mick whispered to no one in particular. Her eyes snapped open. "Who is Judas Iscariot?"

"Shit." I grabbed her hand and pulled her out of the booth. Jack's Place isn't any Garden of Gethsemane, but I know when I'm being betrayed.

Too late. Two bruisers in dark blue suits and ties, dressed for door-to-door bible sales but carrying themselves like they belonged in the ring, came through the front door. Jack's head jerked snake-like in our direction.

I stopped in my tracks and hissed at Mick. "Disappear. Don't argue, just do it." She vanished. Her hand pulled free and she was simply gone.

I cut between tables and met the suits in a relatively open area in front of the bar. The lead man threw up a hand as his partner searched the darkened booths. I took one more step and hooked an inside crescent kick that caught the first man full in the face. His head rocked and he sprawled on the floor. Bar patrons scattered; stools crashed. The second man swung around, one hand jammed inside his jacket. Some bar fly darted between us, scuttling for safety. The air behind the second suit rippled darkly and abruptly Mick materialized for the ambush. Her hands flashed in unison, knife-edges slamming into both sides of the man's neck. The double shuto strike closed both his carotids. Instantly his brain shut down and he collapsed in a heap.

Jack started hollering. The first man struggled to rise. I hopped over, swung a quick, simple roundhouse punch, and there was no more hollering. Jack kept squawking, though. He had a baseball bat in his hand. "God damn you, Murayama, there's no fighting in here! You stay right where you are till the cops get here!"

I walked over to the bar, plenty close enough for him to swing for straight-away center field if he wanted to. "How much did they pay you?"

"I don't know what the fuck you're *talking* about! You're drunk and busting my place up!"

Not yet I wasn't. Mick slipped up beside me and stood wordlessly. I picked up an empty glass and rotated it carefully while Jack kept blathering.

"Who the hell is she, Murayama? Huh?" Perspiration speckled his forehead. "I think she might be UD, that's what I think. You *both* better wait for the cops."

I shook my head affably. "I got other things to do. If I get bothered by the police while I'm doing those things, though, I'll come back and feed that fucking bat to you." I put the glass down and arched a friendly eyebrow. "Understand?"

Jack didn't swing. He didn't do anything. He didn't say anything. Mick tugged at my sleeve, urging me to go. I took her hand and we walked out the door without a backward glance.

"I thought he was your friend," Mick murmured as we headed up the walk.

"He's my bartender. This is the M. Friendship's negotiable." I was running out of both friends and bargaining chips. My apartment had to be under observation and anyone else I did business with would probably be looking to give me up like Jack did. I could think of only one safe place. I pointed to the Tube stop. "South Side," I said. There was only one person I could trust now.

A TRAINING SESSION was in progress on the main floor as we entered the dojo. Hideo Ohta, who'd been a white belt sweeping floors and carrying water when I was at the school led the class in *Goshina kata juniche dan* on Embujo, the main floor, their movements crisp and uniform. Behind Ohta, at the front – in Kamiza, the top seat where wisdom and judgment sit – Master Shiyro observed. Before proceeding farther I bowed to the front and removed my sneakers, gesturing for Mick to do the same. A wooden walkway runs around the main floor and Master doesn't insist on removing shoes unless you walk on the practice floor itself, but under the circumstances I wanted to show as much respect as possible. "Shomen ni rei," I told her quietly. "Bow to the front."

Mick obliged, then slipped out of her canvas shoes and padded behind me as we made our way around the room past Shimoseki, the east side where awards and photographs are displayed, keeping close to the wall. When we reached the old Japanese I bowed deeply. *Sensei ni rei.* "Master."

"Kim-san." No trace of a smile broke his seamed features. His hair and beard were the same wispy white, his eyes sharp and clear as ever. He bowed in return. "It is good to see you."

I gestured to Mick. "This is Mick. A friend. She's... visiting." The old man bowed to her. She replied in kind, bowing deeply though with head and eyes raised to maintain her view of Shiyro. I told him we wanted to talk.

"When class is finished," he said blandly. "It will not be long. Wait in back."

I led Mick to a small gym in rear of the building. We sat on a wooden bench next to a row of grey metal lockers, by the one bearing my name written on a strip of yellowed adhesive tape. I stared at the 65 lb. canvas heavy bag hanging motionless in the far corner.

"Your name is on this door," Mick observed.

I swiveled around and opened my locker. A white jacket and pants hung there, a frayed black cloth belt, my first when I was awarded the rank of shodan. Mick cocked her head, studying the belt. Then her gaze lifted to the top shelf. She reached for the shuriken, but I grabbed her wrist. "Be careful. Those are sharp."

For a long, frozen moment she seemed to be trying to discern if one of them was perhaps *the* shuriken. Then she rose abruptly, dismissing her curiosity. She walked over to the Wing Chun dummy, a cylindrical assembly of polished walnut just over five feet tall with three lengths of smooth, slightly tapered doweling affixed at different angles about four and four and a half feet off the ground. A single "leg" bent at 90 degrees a little over a foot off the floor, the whole affair mounted on slats affixed to the wall, the more modern Gua Jong style having some recoil. Mick laid a hand on it. I joined her. "You familiar with this?" I grasped one of the wooden arms, pushed lightly. The other arms bounced toward her.

Mick's right arm snapped up into a middle block. Her feet shifted subtly, knees bending to lower her weight as her other arm shot down and out, executing a block to a second arm. Her right arm swung down, passing the center line of her body and struck the third arm. Her nostrils flared in a soft, sharp exhalation. I nodded approvingly, suitably impressed. "We have a similar device," she murmured by way of explanation.

No wonder her technique was so good. The practice dummy got little use here, almost none from me over the years, being as I was more interested in Shiyro's Washin-ryu karate. Some of the students dabbled in the Chinese kung-fu style, but it was clear that Mick more than flirted with Wing Chun. I turned up my palms. "Would you care to demonstrate?"

She plucked at her loose black pants, then wagged her head and without further deliberation went to town. She moved with supernatural grace, flowing from a double block into a two-hand shuto strike to the center post, blocking a wooden arm on the recoil, countering the reaction, attacking the torso with linear palm heel and fist strikes, then sliding fluidly into another series of blocks and parries. The dummy shuddered; between blocks she shifted at will and continued to deliver accurate striking attacks with either hands or feet. It wasn't exactly Wing Chun Kung Fu, though it had elements of it. Whatever it was, Mick's performance was incredible. When she finished, she stepped lithely back, panting lightly, eyes bright and expectant. I said, "That was fucking great."

Her eyebrows went up. "I beg your pardon?"

"I said you're fucking great, Mick. Your technique, I mean. You're really good." There was no sign of Shiyro yet and I ventured, "You, ah, want to go a round, maybe? Compare styles."

She cocked her head. "Do you mean fight one another?"

"Spar. Yeah. Don't you do that in training…?"

"We do. As long as we are not enemies, though, you and I."

We certainly weren't that. Despite what I'd witnessed and ignoring good common sense, I changed into my gi. Mick watched without expression and without any apparent discomposure as I pulled off my t-shirt and dropped my pants. Not that she should have been discomfited. Not after the nights in the cottage at Duncan Bay. I climbed into *zubon*, the white pants, donned and tied *uwagi*, the coat, and quickly wrapped my old, frayed black belt around my waist and tied it off. As an afterthought I peeled off my socks and, thus satisfactorily attired in *keikogi*, went to meet Mick on the floor. I didn't really think five and a half feet of brunette Royale would be that serious a challenge. I thought I'd get some light exercise, maybe break a sweat and take some measure of the lady. I got her measure, all right. It was like trying to fight the wind.

The lady kicked my ass.

I don't know how much of our little match Shiyro saw, but after Mick helped me up off the floor for the sixth time I noticed the old man standing by the door. She slipped back, brown eyes wide and alert. Her arms were at her sides, but that didn't fool me one bit. My left shoulder hurt, I didn't think I'd be sitting down for about a week, and my right wrist wasn't broken only because she hadn't wanted to break it. She probably could have broken my neck. "Again?" she inquired deferentially.

"Ah, no." I glanced at Shiyro. "That's good for me today."

She relaxed and nibbled her lip. "You are not hurt, I trust." She was looking past me, at Shiyro. I wasn't hurt, not really. My pride was more bruised than anything.

I grinned and pointed to the shower door. "Go shower up." I gave her a smack on her bottom, half expecting an armlock, but she only gave a good-natured squeak and scampered off. I walked over to Shiyro. His eyes danced with suppressed amusement.

"An interesting young woman, Kim-san," he observed. "She is well trained. I discerned this when you landed on the floor."

"Both times?" I asked casually.

He held up five fingers on one hand, one on the other, and grinned. "All six times."

Naturally. I grinned, too, and rubbed a sore spot on my right hip where an aikido joint-locking technique had landed me.

"So. This young lady. Mick."

"She's-" *A witch*. "-from up north. A client, but we're kind of getting to be friends."

Shiyro grunted. "Is that not bad business?"

"Well, she can't really pay, so it's pro bono, I guess. Kind of a class action thing."

I screwed up my face, wondering. Was I really working for the whole of Isle Royale or was that simple rationalization? Bereft of a decent answer, I exhaled without offering anything more.

"You are sleeping with her," Shiyro said flatly.

"I am not! I mean, we are- we did. But it's not like that."

"Not like what, Kim-san?"

"Like you make it sound." In a world filled with immorality appearances suddenly assumed great import to me.

Shiyro merely smiled and didn't make me answer any more questions. "Go wash, Kim. Then bring your friend for tea."

Mick was waiting, still dressed, studying the shower head protruding from the wall. "There is nothing like this at home." She reached down and smoothly pulled her top off. "Will you show me how it works?"

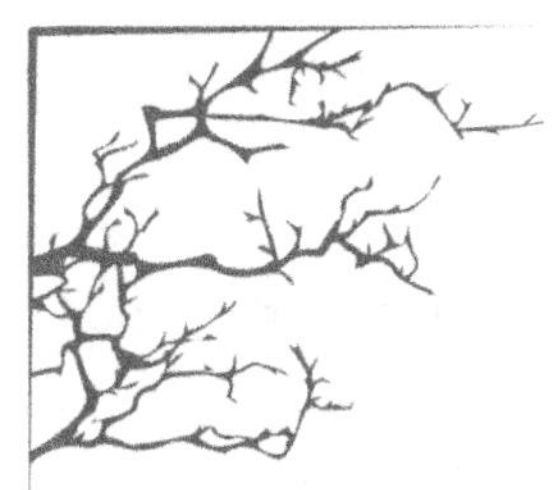

Chapter 13

Tea was served in Shiyro's study off the main floor. I demonstrated for Mick how to kneel by the paper and wood frame door until invited in, then how to enter in a crouch, kneel once more, and slide the door closed. She performed the ritual flawlessly.

The study was spotless, as always, and Sensei had broken out the good china. Water boiled in a kettle set in a small sunken hearth. We sat on tatami for Cha no ryu, the Tea Ceremony. Mick gazed at the single yellow flower in a bamboo vase nestled in a recess in the wall. Behind it hung an oil painting of an eagle in flight, a prowling tiger below. "They're part of the ceremony," I told her. "The eagle and the tiger are symbols of the school."

With deliberate movements Shiyro ladled hot water from the kettle into simple wooden bowls containing matcha, finely ground green tea leaves, then whisked the mixture to the proper frothy consistency before ladling it into small ceramic cups hand painted with green and purple peacocks under an orange sunset. Usually this bores me half to death, but this time it was worth it to watch Mick. She knelt, hands folded in her lap and watched with fascination as the old man went through the complex ritual of making and serving tea with the greatest respect for his guests. For her, anyway. He didn't do it up this big for me. He knew it bored me half to death. Mick accepted the ceramic cup and bowed her head. "Thank you, Mister Shiyro."

"You are most welcome." He handed mine over with a curt, "Here."

We sipped our tea. It tasted like grass clippings, but I kept my mouth shut. Mick didn't grimace or anything. She actually seemed to like the stuff. Polite conversation ensued as is traditional when having guests to tea, Shiyro inquiring of Mick if she were enjoying her visit to the M. She gave me an oblique look. "There are agreeable aspects."

Eventually, with etiquette satisfied, we got down to the purpose of our visit. Shiyro sat with his fingers steepled, listening without interruption as

I explained that Mick was contraband from Isle Royale and my suspicions that Wilmut, Inc. was running a clandestine operation in human trafficking. I gave him the short version of Doc Fredericks' explanation. It seemed ages ago that Doc had peered at the glass slide. I hadn't looked, but that didn't matter. The answers we needed weren't to be found under a microscope. The old master reflected in silence, brow furrowed. At length he said, "You know who is responsible."

"I think so." They were lies hidden in shadows, myth afraid that the world would see them. Shiyro asked, and properly so, if we had gone to the authorities with these allegations. I didn't trust the police and told him so. He accepted that, knowing the M as well as any man. I'd do it myself. "They are the pheasant shut inside," I finished. "I am the hawk who enters to arrest."

"You remember Musashi's words." Shiyro nodded appreciatively. "But be certain your heart is as pure as your words."

I lowered my gaze for a second, then looked up. "I don't know if she's the key to immortality or not, but she ought to be able to live her life without someone cutting it short to their own advantage."

"Revenge is anger," Shiyro said quietly. "Anger clouds the mind and disables the spirit." He knew my heart. He'd walked with me to the alley, stood with me while I cried, the only one who had. Now, he again grasped what I needed. "They will look for you. Use a room in back. I will expect you to earn your keep." Brightening with the decisions made, he added, "If you would care to join us for supper this evening, we are having- spaghetti!"

SHIYRO DOESN'T EAT meat and pasta is a special occasion at the school. We ate with the old master and four of his upper-class dans at a low, black lacquered table, everyone seated cross-legged on tatami. Hideo Ohta, the school's senior black belt, made the introductions – Akiro Kobyashi, James Wantanabe, and a young woman, Lisa Okado, Shiyro's upper-class dans. Everyone nodded politely; Mick bowed her head respectfully to each in turn, then Shiyro signaled that the meal could begin.

We had spaghetti with either marinara or a savory Alfredo, fresh baked bread, and bean curd with soy sauce on the side. Less ceremonial than social, chopsticks were not required and bamboo dishes were eschewed for relatively inexpensive dinnerware – rice bowls and sushi plates with a blue dragonfly motif. There was sake, too, the dry karakuchi still favored by the older, traditional Japanese. I had a cup after the meal. Mick had several. Afterward, she leaned against me as I slid open the door to our austere little room in rear of the dojo. "I like him," she murmured. "Inogi."

Inogi, was it. I stood aside for her to enter. "Master gave you leave?"

"He said I may call him Inogi, yes." Mick walked carefully across the room, arms extended for balance. "I think that the floor is moving, Kim."

I knelt by a trap door in one corner. Straw tatami mats and folded blankets lay neatly stored under the flooring. I hauled them out and began arranging our bedding before Mick fell overboard. She continued to wheel lazily like a red-tail on the breeze. "Hideo looks a great deal like James," she mused. "Do you not think so?"

"They look Japanese," I agreed.

"They both look like you." Mick stopped turning and fixed me squarely. "Did Joanna look like Lisa?"

"No." I sat back on my heels, tongue denting my cheek. "No, Jo didn't look like Lisa."

Mick resumed gliding about the room. I eased down on the tatami with my back to the wall, watching her drift on a rice wine breeze. The sake had more kick than the raspberry stuff on the isle. She stopped and tilted her head back, inspecting the ceiling. "You know, I believe the entire building may be moving. Should we inform Inogi?"

"He's a master of the Way. He sees all. I'm sure he knows there's an earthquake in progress." I extended a hand. "Come here, lady." She accepted with a coy little smile wholly out of character yet at the same time decidedly enticing, and sank down on her knees beside me.

"Was Joanna more attractive than Lisa?" she asked.

"Yeah. She was. To me."

"As you find me more attractive than Jacqueline."

"Yes, Mick. Just like that."

She studied me for another moment, then sat beside me and laid her head on my shoulder. "You do not look exactly like Hideo or James. But even if that were the case I should still find you the more attractive." She cuddled close. Her hair smelled faintly of cleansing rain and cool forests far across distant waters. I slid an arm around her shoulders and closed my eyes, almost back on the island. "Will you ever return?" Mick whispered. "With me?"

Part of me wished I'd never left, that I'd stayed like Dave thought I was being hoodwinked into doing. Another part argued how impossible staying would be. When I didn't answer she lifted her face, oval features obscured by shadow. Her lips were close, breath warm. "Be mine, Kim Murayama." She kissed me softly in the darkness, arms slipping around my neck, pulling me down. "Be mine tonight..."

IN THE MORNING MICK put away our bedding. We swept the room, the hallway, and the small back gym where we'd sparred the previous day. Other students, white and yellow belts, cleaned the main floor and the front porch, sweeping, scrubbing, polishing. Green belts prepared a breakfast of fruit, fish and rice while purple, brown, and some of the black belts meditated or went to temple. Me, I don't go to temple any more. It never does any good. I thought the belief in a Divine Being would be an interesting discussion with a woman of Mick's circumstances, though probably better undertaken at another time.

After chores we went for a bath before breakfast. The small communal affair was deserted. I suspected Shiyro had warned off anyone else contemplating a soak. We undressed in the small antechamber, Mick again evincing no chagrin, then entered the bath room proper where we washed and rinsed thoroughly under a faucet. Rinse water trickled down the floor drain as I stepped into steaming water in the sunken tub. Mick performed the ritual as well, but stood nude, wringing brown hair out as she frowned curiously. "Why do we wash before we bathe?"

"No soap in the tub," I replied tightly. That would be a great offense against the next bather. I gritted my teeth against the almost scalding water as I slid in to my chest; I leaned back, palms resting on the polished wooden rim of the tub, inhaling the long unremembered aroma of smooth, wet Japanese cypress. It had been a long time since I went first, too. I beckoned Mick. "Come on in."

She dipped bare toes that came right back out. "This is very hot."

"Hot as you can stand it." I shifted; water sloshed gently. She screwed up her courage and let herself slowly into the bath. "What do you do on the island?" I inquired.

"Bathe in the lakes."

"Kind of cold in the winter, ain't it?"

"Sometimes we build a fire and heat the water in great black cauldrons," she replied.

Clenched teeth didn't disguise her quip. The water moved as Mick slipped completely in. "It is *very* hot."

"The body is cleaned. Now cleanse the soul."

"Do you think my soul in need of cleansing?"

"Not necessarily." I squinted one-eyed at her through rising vapor. "But a clean soul goes hand in hand with a pure heart and victory goes to the righteous. That's a fact. We'll want to be the cleanest souls with the purest hearts when we go to see Wilmut."

I didn't intend to go into the lion's den just yet, but I wanted to peek through the fence.

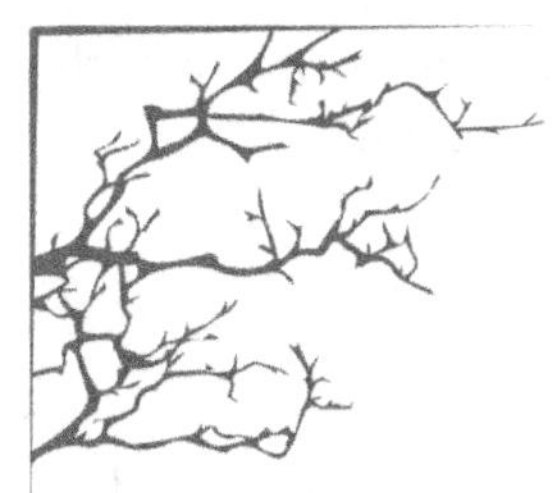

Chapter 14

The Tube let us off three blocks from Wilmut, Inc. across the river on the East Side where the money lives. A quiet tree-lined boulevard took us past a mix of renovated row houses, specialty manufacturing concerns, small upscale restaurants catering to the trendy, and overpriced coffee shops, their outdoor tables already filled by the stylish with-it crowd. I gave Mick a once-over look. Her simple black outfit, while modest by whatever current last-word East Side standards prevailed today, was inconspicuous enough.

"Here does not look like the rest of your city," she opined.

And it's not. You're unlikely to be accosted by cyberpunks who can't afford to keep up with the swank, where stardust and blow are the narcotics of choice, and they aren't done on the sidewalk with caramel chocolate hazelnut lattes and pumpkin spice frappucinos. Over here there's class, see. The cafes charge more for ambiance than they do for coffee, and businesses pay the police to keep it that way on this side of the river. I thought Wilmut probably charged high for their merchandise, too. East Side's where it'd sell.

We walked another block, Mick's hand sneaking into mine. "I fear we will be found out."

I waved aside her concern. "Nobody even knows we're here."

"I am not so certain," she muttered as we drew closer to Wilmut. I could see the company's off-white stucco walls reminiscent of Spanish influence in the Southwest Confederation, topped by slowly rotating cameras, quality digital as opposed to the junk on the city subway. I spotted acoustic sensors mounted higher up, probably infrared somewhere, too. I asked Mick if she could turn invisible for a while.

"I disappear," she replied tersely.

"Right. Will a camera see you?"

"I do not think so." She sounded uncertain about that, but vanished. Her fingers still gripped mine, but she wasn't there. I squinted, looking as hard as I knew how, and still saw nothing. Wilmut's battlements loomed.

I led the way along the walk in front of the compound, glimpsing a dark tinted-glass guard shack just inside the barred entry gate. The main building sat further back, an unpretentious and unremarkable two-story stucco affair surrounded by some smaller, windowless outbuildings, some stuccoed, some cinder-block, all the same off-white. The grounds within were criss-crossed with bright white graveled walks bordered by neatly kept flowers and small topiary bay trees, but otherwise they were empty, as though the place were closed. The air next to me whispered, light as a breeze. "What are we looking for?"

"A way in."

"Do we *want* to go inside?" Mick's tone amply implied that she considered that a Bad Idea.

"I just want to see what's going on in there."

They are killing my sisters her voice growled in my head.

But I had to look. I had to know. I couldn't forget two lakers in a dirty alley a long time ago. If I'd been wrong that night, I never wanted to make the same mistake again.

I understand came subdued, almost apologetic. I squeezed ghostly fingers and kept walking. At the next intersection we turned right, paralleling Wilmut's featureless walls. A camera swiveled, silently tracking us. Further along a service road ran behind the complex and we cut down that under the gaze of more cameras. Tall, old Norway maples guarded both sides of the road casting long, cool shadows. Mick's grip tightened on mine.

Kim... Mounting panic tinged her thoughts now. I frowned, wondering what was the matter, but even as the question coalesced the air grew suddenly oppressive. Saliva filled my mouth. I swallowed twice, trying to catch my breath.

The Darkness. It knows. Please, Kim, let us go away from here.

My stomach lurched once, almost turning over, my head pounding and I was assailed by the nameless fear that I'd felt before on the shore of Duncan Bay. I turned around and started back, pulling my invisible companion after me, but Wilmut's security was better than I'd anticipated. One instant the alley was clear, the next we were hemmed in, four men close in front of us, four more behind. They were well built, wearing moderately expensive suits like the two who had come looking to sell us scripture in Jack's, but unlike the two in Jack's these men were aware, ready and determined. Without conversation or a call to surrender one pulled a compact chromed tranquilizer pistol and fired at me. Sunlight glinted on the stainless steel projectile.

I leaned left, felt Mick's spectral fingers pull free as she went in the opposite direction. The red-tasseled projectile flashed between us and a surprised snarl sounded from behind as the dart found an unintended target.

The Darkness-

Ignore it! I thought fiercely. *Fight. Fight back hard!* I charged the man at the extreme end of their line. He set himself in a defensive stance, hands rising. He'd studied the arts, but he was too slow. I leaped, spinning, and got my foot up over his guard. My heel caught him just above the temporomandibular joint and knocked him out, probably breaking his jaw, too. I heard another man scream in pain. Mick was at work, but there wasn't time to watch. Two stainless steel .45s pointed at me. "Give it up!" one of the gunmen snarled.

"Okay. I'm done." I straightened and brought my hands up, chest high in apparent surrender. I didn't see Mick anywhere, hoped against hope that she'd gotten away.

"Take him, Kersey." The man flicked his pistol. He thought it was over, but he was too close. When he moved, I moved, lunging and slapping the gun aside. It went off, sharp and piercing, but I'd turned sideways and the round flew harmlessly. My right elbow thrust powerfully, all my weight behind it, and smashed the gunman's nose. Blood sprayed and he screamed. The pistol clattered on pavement and he reeled away, hands to his face. I pivoted, crouched low for the next attack, and spun right into 50,000 volts. I know, it's only about 1200 volts delivered, but it feels like 50,000 just the same. The pavement hit me hard, driving the breath from my lungs. Teeth clamped together, I started back up.

"Fucking Slant." A boot hit my chest taking away the rest of my air. I went down again. My opponent waded in, shockstick sparking hot blue.

I WOKE IN COOL DARKNESS but didn't open my eyes. Thick leather straps held my wrists to solid wood chair arms. I sat very still, breathing evenly, and let the effects of the shockstick wear off. At length I lifted my arms ever so slightly, testing the straps. Tight and rugged, they barely stretched. They wouldn't give right away, but when I decided to get up they would. I relaxed once more, waiting. A light snapped on aimed straight at my face, painfully bright even through my eyelids. I winced.

"I thought you were awake," a mild voice remarked.

I opened one eye, squinting against the glare. A shadowed figure, faceless between me and the light, held a smoldering cigarette. Pungent cinnamon curled, a thin, ghostly white stream mixed with dust motes floating in the hard light. "Who are you?" the figure asked.

"Nobody," I managed, my tongue still thick.

"What were you doing outside, Mr. Nobody?"

I blinked watery eyes. "Nothing."

He moved closer, placing the glowing orange tip of the cigarette to the back of my hand. I gritted my teeth as the flesh blackened. It hurt like a bastard, but I didn't make a sound. Straightening, the shadowed man took a slow drag on the bent cigarette and exhaled. "You are very disciplined, Mr. Nobody."

"It was a bitch," I replied tightly, "but I quit. You ought to kick the habit yourself."

"Yes. Offensive, is it not?"

"So's sadism."

"We all have our vices." He commenced a slow walk around the room. Smoke eddied in his wake, the light harsh through the wavering veil. "This place, this city of yours, is filled with vices. It overflows with them, I dare say. Tobacco is but one, and lesser at that." He completed a full circuit and stood before me again, examining the smoldering cigarette between his fingers. "There was a time when I would never... could never have..." He might have meant smoked or tortured people. He smiled to himself without amusement. "There was a time, sir, when many things were not possible. And when many more were. As I say, your city is filled with vices. Who among us is not susceptible? Perhaps before mine overcome me further you will tell me what you were doing outside."

"Just looking. Little something to swap on the street maybe."

"You came here to steal?"

"I dunno'. There's walls and barred doors and guards. Must be something worth something. S'a pharmaceutical factory, right? Pills? Or juice. Maybe P. You got the Power?"

He exhaled smoke from behind me. Cinnamon welled. "You don't strike me as an addict."

"I'm more of a salesman."

"There is nothing like that in here you could sell." Shadow Man paused reflectively. "But of course your streets will buy anything." He came around in front of me again, blocking the worst of the glare. Cigarette smoke haloed around him. "It buys people. Is that what you thought to steal? People?"

"Not in my inventory." With the most trifling movement I rotated my forearms, palms up, hands curling into fists. I lifted, beginning to apply pressure against the leather holding my wrists. "You got stock to move or something?"

This time the smoke was blown in my face. My eyes watered even more, the cinnamon aroma sickening. Shadow Man signaled with a snap of his fingers. A door opened; yellow light slashed across the floor. A man in a suit, probably one of the goons from the alley, bulled through half dragging a smaller figure by one arm. He thrust his captive forward. I almost started as Mick dropped to the floor. Absently inspecting his fingernails in the glare from behind, Shadow Man said more to himself, "As a matter of fact I do have some new stock." He paused, studying me intently, then added, "Mr. Murayama, is it not?"

God damn. I forced myself to remain calm. Mick was alive, though they'd gone rough on her. She crouched on hands and knees, head down, hair loose and disordered, her shirt torn down the front. She stayed silent except for small, labored gasps. Shadow Man regarded her without pity. "Do you know her?"

"No." Rivets held the straps to the stout wooden arms, but I directed my *ki* against them, concentrating the energy of the spirit there. Shadow Man kicked out, getting Mick in the ribs just below her breast. She jerked and bit back a cry. I lunged against my bonds, not trying to break them but more to make known my quarrel with his tasteless comportment. My lunge loosened the straps another couple millimeters, though. "What the hell was that for?"

"I thought you do not know her." He kicked Mick again. This time she let out a yelp and curled tightly into a ball.

"I don't know you, either," I growled, "but I'm not kicking your face in." Yet.

Shadow Man turned slowly, revealing half of an indulgent smile. "You would like to, would you not? Yes. I see that you would." He shoved Mick with his foot. She whimpered softly. "You think yourself capable?"

"Why don't you let me loose and we can find out."

"Fucking Slant." The goon stepped in and landed a solid blow to the side of my face that rattled my teeth. I shook my head, tasting blood. "Shut the fuck up, Slant."

Shadow Man held up a dismissive hand. "Enough, Kersey."

"We got the witch back. We don't need him."

"I said enough." Kersey fell silent at the flat, cold order. Shadow Man addressed me further. "This woman was with you today. She spec-shifted to avoid the cameras. Mr. Kersey is correct. She is a Royale witch." He drew on the increasingly short cigarette, examined the ash, then dropped the butt as he blew smoke. One pointed-toed shoe snuffed out the last feeble orange glow. "Did you honestly think we would not detect a Royale at our own gate simply because she shifted? Are you truly that much of an amateur?"

Apparently I was, though I wasn't about to admit it. Shadow Man reached inside his jacket and withdrew a thin silver case. Opening it, he took out a new cigarette accompanied by the fresh scent of cinnamon. As he closed the case and tapped the filter end on it, a ray of light glinted green from an inlaid stone. He stopped tapping, held the case up. "This? A greenstone. You know it?"

I nodded slowly, trying to focus. Kersey packed a hell of a punch. "I know it."

He returned the silver case to his jacket and lit the cigarette with the flick of a gold lighter. "Is that why you are with her? The stones? Do you buy them from her?"

"No..."

A foot pushed Mick once more. "You think to acquire them through her. Ransom, perhaps. That will avail you nothing."

"No. Jesus Christ."

He resumed pacing. "Perhaps she seduced you. Have you slept with her?" At that Mick uncurled a little, head lifting. Brown eyes regarded me intently through strands of tangled brown hair. A bruise darkened her cheek and there was an abrasion on her forehead, but only determination in her expression. "Have you *slept* with her?" Shadow Man repeated.

"I told you. I've never seen her before."

"Kersey." Another blow rocked me. Flashbulbs exploded behind my eyes and I was thrown sideways in the chair. Shadow Man went on indulgently as though conducting a job interview rather than directing a beating. "They control you, you know. With their looks. Their beauty." He came all the way around and bent. Grabbing Mick's hair, he yanked her head up. She grimaced, but didn't cry out; her gaze remained fixed on me. "Even now she tries. Such sublime pathos. She *is* beautiful, is she not? They all are. Enchanting... even hypnotic. Wretched, lovely little witch." He dropped her. Mick slumped with a barely audible groan. "They control you. With their beauty. Their lies. With sex."

"I don't know her."

"You fucked her." He straightened, blocking the light. I could finally make out his face – rugged features, perhaps chiseled by hard northern winters, hair a distinguished grey neatly barbered, eyes cold as slate. "You fucked her and now she owns you."

I met his stony gaze. "And who owns you?"

At that moment Mick exploded upward with a blood-chilling shriek. "The Darkness owns him!"

Kersey swung around only to catch a spinning kick as Mick came four feet off the floor. Her heel hit him so hard he dropped like a pole-axed steer. Shadow Man turned, too, less surprised but attention nonetheless taken. Abandoning the slow, continuous pressure on the leather straps I poured all my strength into the effort as Mick squared off against our antagonist, eyes flashing. I'd seen her style – she was good, but doubt gripped her, as if bound to fight a battle she knew she couldn't win. Still, she screamed, "I know you, Anton! You are the Darkness! You are treachery and death!"

"And I know you," he chuckled dismissively. "Little Mick, daughter of Theresa, heroine savior of our entire race."

"Your end is appointed!" Mick spat.

"Bold words spoken in a child's voice. But you are no longer ten years old and we are far from the Minong now." After a pause, he added maliciously, "How is Hatchet Lake these days?"

Mick snarled like a wild predator. "I will put you under the waters myself!"

Shadow Man had his back to me, wholly intent on Mick. Clearly he rated her a low-priority threat, and he didn't consider me one at all. That was his big mistake. The buckle on the right strap broke; wood splintered and the left arm tore off the chair altogether. I bounded up, arms high, then both fists crashing down on Shadow Man's shoulders in *kentsui-uchi*, the Hammer Fist. The supra-scapular stun sent tremendous fluid shock surging down both sides of his spine. His legs buckled and he went to his knees, retching wetly.

"He is the Darkness!" Mick cried, still crouched and ready to fight. "He will destroy us all!"

No he wouldn't. I grabbed the back of the chair in which I'd been lashed, tilted it forward, then flipped it, catching it handily by the back two legs and swinging it as I came around. The chair arced high overhead then down, shattering on Shadow Man's skull, shoulders, and upper back driving him face first into the floor. He might have been dead then, but I made certain. I grabbed him by the hair and under the chin, twisted with a sharp motion and snapped his neck with an audible crack. I straightened slowly, quivering all over. Shadow Man lay still, his last smoke smoldering a few feet away. Wisps of cinnamon twisted and curled. I pulled the leather strap and dangling piece of the chair arm off my wrist as Mick dashed over. Chest heaving beneath her torn shirt, she panted, "Is he dead?"

He was supposed to be. Adrenaline receded and my vision began to blur. Balance was becoming a real challenge, but I managed to kneel. There was no carotid pulse. I sat back with a groan. "He's gone, Mick."

She exhaled with relief. "He was the Darkness. Treachery and death."

I was willing to bet he was sterile, too, but before I could ante up the world grew dark. I felt myself leaving the game. Mick caught me, easing me down. I tried to lift my head and failed. "Does he have Joanna's bracelet...?" I mumbled.

"You did not kill the wrong man!" she whispered fiercely. "Not this time." Her fingers dug into my shoulders. "Do you hear me, Kim?"

I could barely see her. Between the shockstick, Kersey's roundhouses and my last all-out effort I was on my way to oblivion. The last thing I heard was Mick's fading voice. "Kim... Kim, you were not wrong. You were not. Take my hand. We must go and it is too far to walk." Grey, soft mist swirled, cushioning me. I floated for I don't know how long until somewhere in dimness I half woke to Mick's forceful voice. "You said we could come here."

"They're after you!" I could picture Doc Fredericks' darting eyes.

"You said if he had nowhere else to go he could come here. I *heard* you. Please. He is hurt."

"I can't."

"Curse you!" Then, softly pleading, "Help him. Help him and I will leave."

Doc hesitated, then growled, "Jesus Christ, all right. Audrey! Give us a hand here. No, not down to exam. Upstairs. I don't want anyone coming in and finding him. Then get Angel."

I tried to sit up to see what was going on, but couldn't. I couldn't keep my eyes open. I was lifted somehow, carried. Mick's fingers clutched my arm, her lips close, breath warm. "I am sorry. I love you, Kim Murayama. I do. That is why I sang to you. You have done no wrong." Her fingers slipped free and her voice receded. "I love you..."

COME THE NEXT EVENING Doc didn't think I was in any shape to leave and maybe I wasn't, but I was ready to go regardless.

"What happened to Mick?" I asked, pulling on my pants. My head still hurt, a low-grade pounding behind my eyes, especially when I bent forward.

Doc leaned against the wall beside the door, scowling, arms folded in his wrinkled, dull white lab coat. "I don't know what happened to her."

"Horseshit, you don't." I reached for my shirt folded on the back of the room's only chair.

"Horseshit yourself, Murayama." He pushed off the wall. "She dumped you here and took off."

I was kind of afraid that's what had happened. I'd hoped it would've gone another way, but I wasn't all that surprised. I looked around. "Where the fuck are my sneakers?"

"Under the bed," Doc said. "Look, the witch said you went to Wilmut..."

I bent to retrieve my sneaks, blinking back a wash of dizziness as I sat up on the edge of the bed to pull one on. I grimaced up at him. "Wilmut's cloning them. For the telomerase. Like you figured."

"What do you mean like *I* figured?" He swallowed apprehensively as if credit for figuring it that way would be A Bad Thing. Which it could be if the clinic went up in flames like Dave's office had. "God damn it, I told you not to go digging up trouble, Kim. Is anything coming back on me? On the clinic, I mean."

I doubted it. There was no army of mad scientists, no horde of pirate kidnappers plundering the Great Lakes, no conspiracy of evil. Conspiracies are mostly 98% bullshit, anyway. The remaining 2% is entertainment. Or business. In this case telomerase – clandestine, unethical and ruthless to be sure, but still basically just business. The company wouldn't want a scandal. They wouldn't want the authorities involved. That would just muck up everything and cost everybody money. I pulled on my other sneaker, squeezing my eyes shut and wishing my headache would go away.

"I don't think you're going to have any trouble," I told Doc. "Anton's gone." Him and his cinnamon cigarettes. My nose wrinkled at the distasteful memory. I could still smell it blowing in my face.

"Mr. Anton, you say." Doc licked his lips. He didn't want to be involved, but his uneasy curiosity won out. "I don't think I've heard of him. Is he in the medical field?"

"Not any more." I snugged the last laces tight and sat back on the bed. My head still hurt, but not as bad. "He was a Royale working for Wilmut."

Doc's eyes widened; I almost smiled. If Mick or any of her sisters don't want to be seen, you won't see them. Only another Royale could ever find them, much less catch one on that freaking island, the way he snagged Mick and me outside Wilmut. All the stories? They weren't half of it. Hell, I didn't know half of what there was to know and I damn sure knew ten times what everybody else does or thinks they know. I let out a shaky breath, unable to repress the taste of super-heated air scalding my lungs, the pain of scorched skin. I looked down at the cigarette burn on the back of my hand. It was nothing compared to Mick's past that was my memory now, too. I stood, a trifle unsteady, leaning on the small bedside table. "They're not gonna' push it."

"It's not that simple. This won't be the end of it." Doc seemed to debate with himself. His jaw worked, then, with a dispirited chuckle he lowered himself onto the old slat-back chair by the bed. His lab coat hung as worn and tired as he looked. "I warned you to drop it. I begged you."

"You never begged me."

"Shut up. Just... shut up. I should have kept quiet when you brought her in here and I shouldn't be talking now, but it's too damn late so just shut up and listen."

I obliged and did both. He launched into a lecture that at first struck me as evasive – how Mick was made by removing the nucleus of a somatic cell, say a skin cell from another Royale's arm, and transferring it into an unfertilized egg emptied of its DNA, donated by another Royale whether she wanted to donate or not. Once that concoction became an early-stage embryo in a test-tube it was implanted into the womb of an adult or almost adult female whether she wanted to be a mom or not. The manufactured Royales then became additional cell donors, surrogate mothers and, more importantly, rich sources of telomerase for God blessed never die immortality that supposedly didn't work. Doc didn't know how the telomerase was extracted, how it was administered to a client or how that whole program was carried out. He didn't know what the process did to the donor. "I didn't work in that area," he finished lamely.

I scowled. I think I'd always suspected, subconsciously. He didn't know everything about the witches of Isle Royale, no, but he knew an awful lot about cloning.

Seeing my expression he grated, a little defensively, "I was just out of med school. I was broke and they were paying for lab researchers. I was there a couple of years, then the world fell apart. Everything fell apart and now I'm here."

"And Wilmut's on the East Side making telomerase factories."

"They're not going to quit just because you went by." A heavy sigh weighted with guilt preceded further admission that he'd been holding back. "They can make a viable embryo almost every time. A whole person. Browns, Golds, Blacks, Greens... did you see any of the green-haired ones?" He didn't wait for an answer. "Somebody playing wigsnatch during base work just to see if it could be done. Anything they want can be programmed and..." Marking my expression of dawning realization, he trailed off. "What...?"

I stared at him with the sudden, horrified understanding of Mick's fateful words: *I shall not live half so long as you.* I should have guessed. I should have fucking *known*. "When are they programmed to turn off?" I growled. "When does she die?"

He looked at me in silence for a few seconds, then put his head back and closed his eyes. "Around thirty years old. Twenty-nine, thirty. Maybe thirty-one if she's lucky."

About the end of her prime child bearing years. I wanted to hit him. I wanted to lash out at Wilmut, the contemptible presumptions, barbaric treatment, all of it, but I held my temper in check for the moment.

"Their cells stop working," Doc went on. "All of them, all at once. The brain cells stop secreting neuro-transmitters. The axons don't carry transmissions, the dendrites don't fire... the heart doesn't get the message any more and quits beating. They just stop living." He shrugged helplessly. "I understand it's painless."

"Really. You ever have all that happen to you?" Of course he hadn't. He looked away, as he damn well ought to. I shook my head. "Anton was a Royale. He was fifty-five if he was a day. Maybe sixty or better."

"There's a fifth type," Doc said miserably. "A few. Grey hair, grey eyes. Engineered somehow to live longer. I don't know how. I wasn't *in* that section. I've had occasion to treat a witch or two since then, that's all. They find their way here sometimes, like yours did with you, and I keep my God damn mouth shut. I learned enough with the company to convince me that shutting up was the way to go. That's what you ought to be doing. They know who you are, Kim. That's bad. Very bad."

"Not as bad as it's going to be when they get to know me better." I started for the door. "Thanks for everything." The forced expression of gratitude left a sour taste on my tongue.

"Let it go!" Doc called after me. "It doesn't matter any more!"

I paused in the hall, looking down the stairs. Doc's charge nurse Angel stood on the landing, gripping the banister, her expression anxious. I don't think she'd ever heard Doc and I at odds before. Watching her, I replied evenly to Doc's assertion. "It does matter."

"She's gone, Kim," he insisted. "She's on a boat and gone."

I smiled to myself. Mick the Witch wouldn't take a boat back to Isle Royale. She'd ride the mists, grey and soft out of nowhere to the land of the impossible. I thumped downstairs past Angel and out into the bleak night.

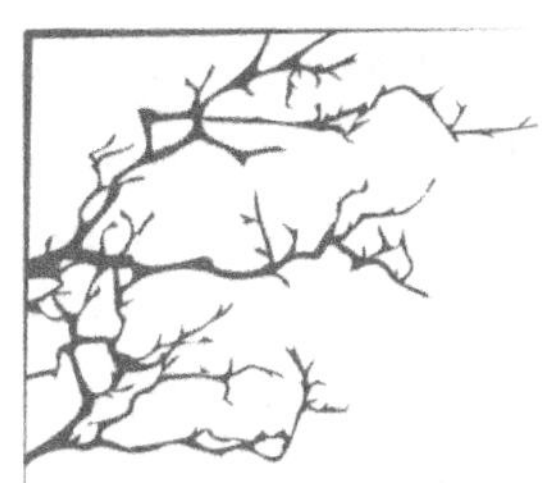

Chapter 15

For a time I wandered aimless and brooding. I considered returning to Wilmut and demanding names – beating people until I got them – but rejected the idea as sheer bravado. I wouldn't get past the front gate. I thought about going over to Jack's and finishing my beer, then shoving his baseball bat down his throat while asking *him* for names, but this, too, I decided against. Jack took money to make a call, probably to a broker who advised the company, nothing more. He didn't know the players or anything about the real game, only how to make a B. Doc probably didn't know who the real players were, either. Anton likely did, but he wouldn't be talking.

I wandered some more, then changed my mind and did go to Jack's. I only had a beer, though. I didn't shove anything down his throat or even ask him a question. Shaking so bad he slopped foam on the bar, Jack set me up with one on the house.

I drank, hardly tasting it. When I finished I eschewed using my plate, leaving a wad of the bills Dave had given me on the bar and walked out, ignoring Jack's insistence that I needn't pay. The Canadian Bobbys were worth three times as much as the beer cost and might keep his mouth shut for a while. Or not. I wasn't particularly concerned either way.

On the walk I stood in weak, watery yellow light, holding the roll of Bobs in my hand. I hadn't bought Mick any clothes. She still wore the loose black outfit. She didn't need any more. I looked at the money, an image of thirty pieces of silver drifting through my thoughts. What did *I* need? Love? I never did tell Mick that I loved her. And what difference had I? We doomed one another.

I slipped the bills in my pocket and resumed walking, hands shoved in my pockets as I wandered down nameless cross streets, past grimy tenements leaking music, laughter, arguments, paying little attention to where I was or where I was going until the soft whisper of tires approached from behind. I held my stride, pushing my thoughts, questions and doubts away, clearing my mind. The black limousine drew abreast, matching my pace as the smoked glass rear window powered silently down. I slowed to a halt and the car eased to the curb. A man leaned forward, head turning.

"Mr. Murayama." I judged him in his sixties, tan and trim with a full head of salt and pepper hair neatly barbered. He wore a tasteful dark blue suit over a crisp white shirt and a maroon tie, the whole effect exuding the well-manicured air of affluence and understated power. I checked up and down the walk – not a soul in sight – but this wasn't an attack. Not yet, anyway or I'd already be fighting. Mr. Manicure wanted to chat.

"Kim Murayama." I gave him a polite, if curt, nod. "That's me."

"My name is Spahn. Wallace Spahn. I'm on the board of Wilmut. Won't you join me?" The door swung open, the parlor beckoning the fly.

I shook my head. "I get carsick. Why don't you come out here?"

Spahn hesitated, then smiled the way people do when humoring a recalcitrant child. He climbed out and I could see his black leather Oxfords, the kind of footwear that goes for four figures or I was a macaque's uncle. I had a hunch that it had been a long time since he actually worked the concrete himself. I was willing to bet he looked a lot younger than he really was, too. He straightened his suit coat, offering me that same smile. "I've been hoping to meet you, Mr. Murayama. We have a lot in common. More than you might think. I'd like to offer you a membership in our...fraternity."

I doubted I had anything in common with this guy, but all I said was, "I understand it's a fairly select club. Probably expensive, huh?"

"For you there would be no charge. A trial membership, if you will. No fee, though we would ask for certain considerations."

"How about if I stop nosing around and upsetting your apple cart?"

"That would do nicely."

"Well..." I tugged my earlobe. "I don't know, boss. Don't know if my conscience'll let me do that. See, none of this should have happened. My buddy Dave, he shouldn't have got jammed up, I shouldn't have got jammed up... You shouldn't be monkey-fucking around with people's DNA and jamming everybody up 'cause it just ain't right, you know? But everything's all jammed up and, well, here we are." I lifted one shoulder carelessly.

He glanced briefly into the limo, the crocodile smile fixed in place, but that didn't fool me. He wasn't standing on Shit Street gabbing with me because he liked the ambiance. This was slumming; it was galling him just to be here, but he wanted something bad enough to get his hands dirty. I edged to one side, putting him between me and the driver's compartment, and said, "Do us both a favor. Just come on out with it and never mind the slipdick."

"Very well. You're direct, as I knew you would be, if rather plebeian." Sticks and stones. I didn't give two shits if he was insulted or what he thought. "The witch, then. She can be yours."

I had to smile. "Until she's thirty years old."

"As long as you want, Mr. Murayama." His eyes narrowed, calculating, and his voice dropped. "If I order it, as long as you want." Softly, persuasively, Spahn delivered his sales pitch. As easily as she was made to die, Mick could be remodeled. The inevitable could be changed. I started to ask if it were true, but clamped it off. It had to be a lie. This wasn't a chance to make up for the past, to be on time and be a hero. "I can give you both a better life than you ever dreamed possible," Spahn finished. Mick could live forever. I could live forever. Beyond weak street light a few stars winked on through a thin overcast. I thought I saw Draco looking down on us.

"No," I told him then.

"You're rejecting my offer?" His brows drew down. "You do realize we can exterminate her."

"And you should realize," I replied casually, examining my nails some more, "that I can break your God damn neck just like I did your buddy Anton's. Your driver may get me with the gun he's trying to aim in there, but you're in the way just now-" I glanced up. "If you try to move I *will* break your neck. Right here on the sidewalk. Right now."

Spahn had started to shift, but checked. "Do you really think you can do that?"

"I know I can."

"You condemn the witch to death," he murmured.

He'd already done that in a test tube. Across the way on the opposite walk a group of streeters gathered at the mouth of a dark alley. I couldn't tell what gang these were or if they were free agents, didn't really care. They were just more cheap help Spahn had hired. Another black sedan slid around the corner, lights doused as it rolled quietly to a stop. Those wouldn't be amateurs.

"I don't want to see you killed," Spahn said with fake bonhomie that just pissed me off more. "If we wanted that you'd already be dead."

"I don't want to kill anyone, either," I told him frankly. "If I did, *you'd* already be dead." I jerked a thumb at his ride. "Tell your boy to put away the gun and you can get going."

Spahn seemed about to say more, then must have concluded against it. He gestured dismissively into the car, then got back in and closed the door. Before putting up the window he looked at me. "Good-bye, Mr. Murayama. I doubt that we'll see one another again."

"Let's hope." The car pulled smoothly away. I watched it, hands on my hips, then looked across the way. The streeters, a dozen or more, moved forward with malignant determination. I kind of figured that was what Spahn had meant when he said we wouldn't be getting together again.

The second black sedan lurched into motion, lights flaring as it accelerated. Just up the way on my side a narrow alleyway beckoned between two decrepit project housing buildings; I raced for it before I got cut off, sprinting through the dark and pungent garbage. The alley was too narrow for the car. High beams blazed from behind, throwing my dancing shadow long and thin ahead of me, the horn blaring angrily. The engine roared and the lights swung away; voices yelled and cursed, footsteps pounding down the alley in pursuit. Rounding the corner of one apartment house I ran down a crumbling, buckled blacktop strip paralleling a chain link fence on one side, overflowing dumpsters backed up to the building on the other. A dark, abandoned factory crouched beyond the fence and I was about to go over when I got blindsided. The streeter crashed into me with a yell, grabbing me in a bear-hug and shouting hoarsely. "I got him! I got him!" And he did have me. For a few seconds.

I bent my knees, lowering my weight, and stomped hard. My heel broke bones in the streeter's foot. He let out a howl, but hung on. That was okay with me, too. I snapped my head to the rear, smashing into his face and breaking his nose. Blood gushed through a wet scream. His grip loosened, but he still didn't let go. I brought my foot up sharply behind me, between his legs, and then he let go with a painful grunt. As he staggered, clutching his groin, I twisted sharply at the waist, executing a short, powerful elbow strike to the rear. *Empi uchi* got him in the temple, dropping him like a stone. Free, I leaped toward the fence with a quick look back. The kid was maybe eighteen, twenty years old, earrings in his nose and eyebrows, hair spiked and dyed purple. That last might have been genetic instead. He could have swallowed mods and turned himself purple all over if he wanted to. Not that I cared. I did wonder if he knew why he was after me, if he bothered to ask who paid him or if it was just another stick-smoke lark in a life without purpose. Did he wonder now that he was bleeding and half crippled?

Air moved behind me, head high. I bent forward quickly; board crashed into chain link, shaking and rattling the fence. Still bent, I shot a kick to the rear, *ushiro-geri* burying the ball of my foot in my attacker's solar plexus. He folded and went down retching; his weapon, a bladeless hockey stick, clattered. I grabbed it up as the first of the pursuing pack reached me and sprang, whipping the stick up, the long end rising in an underhand strike, much like drawing the sword from the kneeling position. The streeter was charging hard, moving into my attack, and the end of the stick caught him solidly under the chin. His head snapped back, ponytail flying, and he went down, skidding sideways like a base runner sliding home under the throw. I'd tagged him, though, and he was out at the plate.

Another one, bald as a baby's ass with eyeballs as opaque as full blown cataracts came next. He got the long end of the stick, too, as it described a quick loop and whistled in from the other direction. There was a loud crack and blood sprayed. The kid screamed, staggering aside and clutching his hairless head. A third skidded to a halt, neon reds wide in alarm. He put up his fists as if to do battle, then muttered, "Shit... fuck this" before turning and running back the way he'd come. So much the better. The hunters drew near. Time for this fox to be off.

I chucked the stick and scrambled up the shaky, swaying chain link fence. Grabbing at the top I hauled myself into a vertical handstand, unmilled wire ends cutting my palms as I vaulted over. I landed in a crouch and immediately ran toward the looming factory. The fence shook violently, angry voices swearing and threatening. I didn't look back. It was perhaps a hundred yards across twisting cracks and fissures in crumbled blacktop to the factory. Clumps of weeds sprouted around rusted hulks of abandoned cars between leaning, unlit light poles. I double-quicked, careful not to twist an ankle or worse.

Half way there the black sedan roared into the lot, headlights swinging round to lock on. I angled away, still making for the factory, but the car was much faster. Twin exhausts booming, it cut me off. I doubled back, zig-zagging in the gloom. The streeters at the fence, realizing my predicament, set to howling and pointing. Fists shook and more than one knife was brandished, yet for all the clamor no one scaled the fence to come and get in on the play. I jogged along the fence line, breathing effortlessly, looking for a way out. My antagonists followed, secure behind chain links, jeering as the sedan closed in.

I stopped, exhaled, then turned to face the car. High beams blazed, brilliant and dazzling. I stood my ground, fingers curling into fists sticky with blood oozing from my palms, gauging the closing rate of the car. It didn't slow. As the streeters shrieked madly, I charged. Three strides and I took off, tucking one leg beneath me and extending the other in a flying side-kick – *yoko tobi geri*. I kind of wished Master Shiyro had been there to see it. It was almost perfectly timed. My foot struck the car's windshield an inch or two higher than I'd intended, but good enough. Safety glass shattered into thousands of tiny, diamond fragments. My forearm took a bruising hit on the leading edge of the car's roof as my foot drove into the front compartment, tearing the steering wheel in half and crashing into the driver's chest. I had a brief impression of him – young, well built, an expensive suit like Kersey's – then my moving mass and the hurtling momentum of the vehicle delivered a devastating blow. My leg shuddered and I felt his sternum break. Fluid shock ruptured his heart; he probably died before he realized what had happened.

The car careened wildly to the left with me still half in and half out of the shattered windshield. The front seat passenger shouted in dismay. I rolled onto my side and snapped a roundhouse kick that took him in the face, smashing his nose. More blood sprayed, more shouting erupted from the back seat, but I scrabbled clear, balancing in a crouch on the hood as the car slowed. Before it stopped I jumped to the inside of its turn, hit the ground and rolled. I came up at a run, dashed in again as the left rear passenger door flew open. A leg emerged, patent leather shoe searching for purchase, and a hand appeared with a pistol pointed at the night sky. Still moving I leaped again, spinning 180 degrees to execute the flying spinning back kick. My foot hit the door, slammed it closed on the arm. Bone cracked and the man screamed, dragging his arm back in as the gun tumbled away. I landed and ran after the sedan, bent double as it rolled slowly to a halt. The right rear door opened and a fourth man sprang out. I crouched at the rear bumper, hidden by the rise of the trunk lid.

"Where is he?" the man yelled. I recognized the voice.

"Jesus Christ, I don't know," from inside the car. "He broke my God damn nose."

"Frank's dead! He came right through the fucking windshield and fucking killed Frankie!"

Impatient, the fourth man now stormed round the fender. "What are those God damn useless street fucks doing?" It was Kersey, as I'd thought, and this time it was my turn. I exploded like a bomb right in his face, grabbing his gun hand, stepping in close and driving an elbow strike into his mouth. Breaking teeth tore my jacket and shirt, skinned my elbow. Simultaneously I yanked, tearing the pistol free from his suddenly nerveless fingers, and slammed a knee into his thigh. *Hiza-ate* blasted the common peroneal nerve. That leg gave out and sympathetic reaction collapsed the opposite one as well. He was on his way down, but I helped him with a palm-heel strike to the chest, driving him that much harder into the unyielding asphalt. He lay stunned and bewildered.

I stepped alongside, transferring his appropriated .45 automatic from my right hand to my left. I regripped it and aimed at his head. Blood smeared the hard plastic grips. "Hey," I said blandly. My breathing was barely above normal. I think it unnerved Kersey.

He stared for a moment, uncomprehending, then focused. "Fuck you," he spat through frothy red saliva. A hunk of broken enamel fell free and skittered across black pavement. "We shoulda' killed you and sunk you in the lake like I wanted."

"You probably should have," I agreed. The car moved, rocking on its shocks. The front passenger door came open and I pulled up, firing in the same motion. The gun bucked, nearly jumping out of my blood-slick hand. The man, nose swollen, eyes purpling, was slammed against the open door. His dress shirt puffed as the round impacted his chest, his features contorting in a gasp drowned out by the deafening crack of the shot, and I saw his pistol coming up. I don't know if he had a spiderweb vest or not. At that exact instant I thought he did, or that his shirt was spun from the synthetic ballistic thread. I thought he was going to keep fighting despite being hit. Before that moment I hadn't intended to shoot anyone, but in a flash everything changed.

I fired again. The bullet exploded out the back of his head showering brain and bone across the glossy black hood. As he sank lifeless to the ground I shifted, letting go of the gun with my left hand and grabbing for it with my right. Snatching it in mid-air I thrust it into the open rear door and pulled the trigger four times. I didn't know if the man with the broken arm had spiderweb, either, or even if he had a gun. I know he screamed when he was shot. After that there was nothing but the incessant ringing in my ears. I glared at Kersey sprawled at my feet.

"Fucking Slant!" Blood filled his mouth. His nails clawed pavement and he struggled to sit up. "You're dead! You're fucking dead! Your witch whore, too!" His pistol dangled in my hand. "You want to use that?" He managed to sit up. "Huh? You want to kill me so I can't waste your whore?"

I looked at him, my expression blank. Exhaust puffed from the tailpipe of the black car. After a few seconds I turned and started to walk away.

"I'll kill her!" Kersey shouted through broken teeth. "I'll fuck her and make you watch, you son of a bitch!" That was when I stopped. He kept screaming. "I'll fuck her till she dies!"

I stopped, looking down at the gun in my hand. "No," I whispered to the night. "You won't."

The .45 went off one more time and it was finally quiet.

None of the streeters wanted to play any more. Varicolored neon eyes watched in silence as I walked slowly toward the fence. As I drew closer they edged away, slipping off by ones and twos, then scattering like cockroaches. I guess they thought I was a lot more dangerous than I felt. I was glad after all that Shiyro hadn't witnessed my performance. Hell of a show, yeah, but nothing to be proud of. I crossed through a break in the fence and headed for the main drag. Along the way I slipped Kersey's pistol down a storm drain. Even if it were found, the police couldn't link it to me. Unless they ran DNA tests on the blood, of course, and matched it with my service record.

Wouldn't that be ironic?

UNBIDDEN, MY FEET TOOK me to the dojo. A few oil lamps still burned and the house guard passed me with no mention of my dirtied clothes, the caked blood on my hands and arms. Shiyro looked up from a scroll as I was ushered into his study.

"Sensei." I bowed stiffly.

"It is late." The old man took in my appearance. "What has happened?"

"A disagreement. A bad one."

He nodded, lips compressed. To the house guard he said tightly, "Bring water to wash. And salve for cuts." He gestured to the tatami opposite him across the low table. I crossed to the mat, folded my legs and sank down with a dispirited sigh. "What sort of disagreement, Kim-san?"

They wanted me dead. I didn't want to die. I told him what had happened – Wilmut, Doc's clinic, the deal Spahn offered me and what happened in the empty, broken parking lot. What I'd done. Shiyro listened intently, not interrupting. The house guard returned with a bowl of warm water, several cloths, and a pasty disinfectant mixture that he used to clean my cuts. Dried blood wiped away, he wrapped my wounds, then withdrew.

"Immortality." Shiyro contemplated the idea, pouring us some tea in small ceramic cups. "Interesting. I would not have thought it possible. And he offered Mick life."

"Yes." I hung my head. "I refused."

"I would have been sorely disappointed had you chosen otherwise. Where is your lady friend now?"

"Gone." I shrugged listlessly. Home, I supposed. The island. She wanted Anton dead, I killed him – killed quite a few people – and then she left. I wished that wasn't the M.O., that instead it was what I thought when she kissed me, when she held me and I didn't see Joanna in my dreams anymore because Mick was there instead. I probably should have said something when she told me she loved me, but... no. It was all bullshit and I sucked for it. I gritted my teeth. She'd used me.

After a prolonged silence Shiyro murmured, in a way that didn't necessarily need an answer, "Do you love her?"

I stared at my hands, slowly turning the small teacup. A peacock flew gracefully in a glossy blue ceramic sky. After a lengthy silence I climbed to my feet, my decision made, and bowed politely. "Thank you, sensei." He didn't reply. Didn't need to. We'd been down this path before. I went to my locker in the back gym where the shurikens waited.

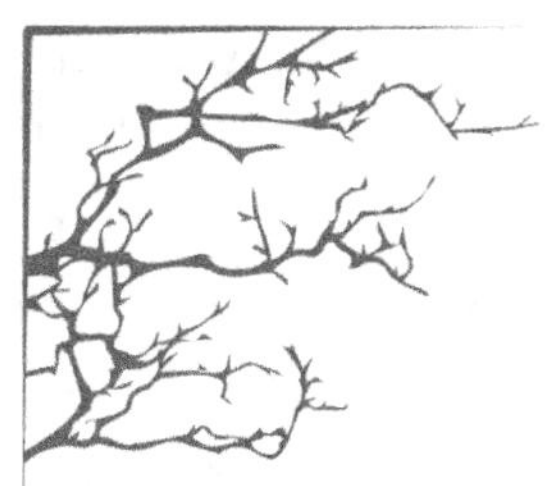

Chapter 16

I had to find Dave. I stalked the waterfront checking dive watering holes without success. I didn't bother with the crack joints. Dave doesn't do that shit. I didn't expect to see his shingle hung on some other warehouse, either, and I didn't.

Under heavy clouds the bay lay still, silent lake freighters floating well out, strange sea creature silhouettes on oily black water. I stopped at a piling occupied by a dozing gull. The grey-mantled bird pulled its head from beneath its wing and gave me a sleepy look. I eyed the red spot on its beak and asked, "You know where the Shady Lady is?"

"I sincerely doubt a herring gull will be able to answer that question, Mr. Murayama."

I turned slowly, the hairs on the back of my neck standing up in a familiar fashion. The heretofore silent Royale from Duncan Bay the night Mick sang to me regarded me without expression. Her full-bodied raven hair surrounded her pale features like a hood, giving her the appearance of a pallid, scowling female version of the Grim Reaper. I said, "Aimee, isn't it?"

She nodded, her eyes two black marbles set in alabaster. "I have been looking for you. You are difficult to find."

"Kind of like being invisible."

"Do I detect a note of sarcasm?"

"I don't know. Do you?" I scowled and ladled out some more in case she needed a second helping. "Let me guess. You've been kidnapped, but you've run away and need my help to get home again."

"You *are* being sarcastic."

Jesus, she was perceptive. "I can't help you. Good night." I turned and started away. I'd had just about all of the Royales I could take for one lifetime. Anton was dead, the job was done. I didn't want to be used any more.

"The Darkness is gone from this place," Aimee called after me, "but only for a time. Do you not think they will send their shades again? Do you not think the Darkness will take its revenge upon Mick? Upon us all?" She caught up to me, grabbing my arm and pulling me to a stop. "Do you think it cannot visit its wrath on you here?"

She could have been their agent for all that, could have pulled a gun or a knife and done the job. Maybe she could have.

"I am not-" Aimee came up on her toes, anger flaring before she regained control and sank back. "I am not the Darkness."

I didn't really care what she was or wasn't, whether she knew what I thought of her or not. I brushed her hand away and started off once more. She grabbed my arm again. I stopped and said quietly, "Let go of me."

She hung on, fingers digging in. "Do what you will, Mr. Murayama, but hear me first. Mick is in peril for exposing Anton. She has fled your great city to save you. She has chosen her own death instead of yours."

I couldn't bring Mick back from the dead. If she was at the bottom of Lake Superior there wasn't a fucking thing I could do about it, though I doubted that was the case. Mick the Witch wouldn't be so easily undone. I kept my expression and, I hoped, my thoughts carefully neutral, repressing a smile as the eastern sky began to lighten behind the lifting clouds. The first thin rays touched my face like warm fingertips in the cool morning air. "The job's finished," I said. I pulled free of the dark witch and walked off. The herring gull stood, ruffling its feathers as I passed. Aimee didn't follow.

Once it grew light enough I spotted the *Lady* at anchor about a half mile out in the bay, back-lit by brilliant orange as the sun burned through. A clammer untying from a rickety, waterlogged dock agreed to take me out for 15B up front. I paid him with a 20 Bobby and told him to keep the change, making him even happier to give me a lift. I crouched between the thwarts as the under-powered outboard labored and smoked. O'Connor stood on the flying bridge and answered the hail as we drew alongside. He dropped down to meet me, one powerful arm hauling me aboard with ease.

"Thanks, man," I told him as my ride chugged off. "Dave on board?"

"He's in the galley." I started below and O'Connor added, "He's not alone."

Not all that surprising. I ducked through the door and dropped down. Dave sat at the table, a mug of black coffee cooling in front of him. Aimee stood to one side, expression blank.

"Murayama." Dave stared at me with bloodshot eyes. After a long moment he hooked a thumb over his shoulder in the direction of the small stove. "Want a cup?"

Before I went for it, I gave the dark Royale a smug little smile. "Told you I could find it."

"SO WHY ARE YOU REALLY going back, Dave?" I sipped coffee and watched the sun glitter on the rippling surface of Lake Ontario as Dave tilled us west. "Don't throw me overboard for asking, but you know what they say."

"They're making me do it, right?" He chuckled grimly. "I thought you didn't buy that shit."

"I thought you did." I wasn't sure precisely why Dave was letting Aimee stay on board – he'd been pretty insistent that he didn't want Mick or any other witches on his boat ever again – and some sinister coercion would account for this about-face. I let it slide. There was no point in that debate any more.

Dave was indisposed to talk game, either. He stared off to the horizon, brow knit, fingers tight on the wheel. "I been having these dreams about Sena. They start almost as soon as I close my eyes. Last night she was burning and I heard her scream. It was so fucking real it woke me up." He turned haunted eyes on me. "That been happening to you?"

I shook my head. "I haven't been dreaming about Sena, no."

"I mean about Mick, you dumb fuck."

I hadn't, nothing like what Dave described, but I was being drawn back to the island just as he was. I had a reason for allowing it to happen, though.

We made the Welland Canal, transiting without difficulty, and Dave held the *Shady Lady* on a straight course southwest through Lake Erie. We passed off Long Point and after that didn't see close land again until we rounded Point Pelee just shy of the Detroit River. The *Lady* made good headway, averaging 25 knots in open water, and we started up toward Lake St. Clair barely twelve hours after clearing the canal. We had to reduce speed in the dark and smoke pouring from Dead Detroit, but Dave still made good time and before dawn we passed Sarnia bound for Lake Huron. I estimated another eight to ten hours before we made the North Channel. We scrubbed the decks again, working in silence, each of us consumed with his – or her – own thoughts. I made myself not look at Aimee scouring forward of me and kept my mind as empty as possible, concentrating on my strokes, the bristles' rasp as my arm moved mechanically. Dirty black water ran around my knees, off the deck and into the lake. Afterward I had something to eat and laid down in my cabin. I did my best to stare at the ceiling and not think about anything. Eventually I dozed off. I'd like to say I don't know where the dream came from, but I do.

It came from dim, remote forests of unsullied pine, invisible mystery riding cold north winds across night waters. With the night and sleep it came bringing shadow images of a young brunette running toward something even more horrible than what she ran from. It brought images of charred timbers and cold ashes, lightning flashes beyond distant thunderclouds, of irresistible doom taking shape. I ran, too, trying to catch her, unable to gain, knowing I couldn't. Knowing what it led me toward I ran anyway until icy blackness closed in, the Darkness coming down around me.

I woke, sweating in the cool emptiness of my cabin. The *Lady* remained underway, undeterred, engines drumming steadily. I lay for a time, breath slowing as my perspiration cooled. At length I rose and went on deck. The night lay cloudless, cold starlight glittering from that hard black sky. I lifted my eyes to the heavens, searching, and at length turning my gaze north. I stood for a long time, just looking and listening. I thought I heard faint lyrics, the echoes of memory sung around a far bonfire in a distant clearing.

I didn't sleep the rest of the way, not wanting to dream and wary of who might hijack my unsupervised thoughts. O'Connor said Aimee wanted to talk to me, said she thought I was dodging her. I let her keep looking and kept my feelings corralled, drinking black coffee in the galley and staring out the porthole or hanging out on the bridge drinking more coffee, staring at the lake or at Dave. I was tired by the time we transited the Soo Locks and Dave was exhausted, eyes red-rimmed, knuckles white on the wheel. He needed to rest, but he wouldn't listen to me. It didn't matter. None of us were going to rest until we came to final terms with Isle Royale. I left the bridge, dropping down the ladder to the main deck. It was cool and I took a moment to button up my old denim jacket, patting the shuriken stowed in the inside pocket, then went and stood at the bow, watching the home stretch draw near.

ISLE ROYALE CAME INTO view shortly before 5:00 pm, the weather further deteriorated from cool and dull an hour out of Sault Ste. Marie to cold winter grey. Superior grew rough, three- to five-foot swells slowing the *Lady's* speed. She barely averaged 20 knots and night closed in by the time O'Connor lowered the marine glasses and announced, "Palisades off the port bow."

Dave cranked the wheel hard to port. The *Lady* heeled over, slamming into waves as she cut sharply toward the island. Everyone lurched, grabbing for handholds and leaning to starboard until the ship came back on an even keel. Dave's nostrils flared and he glared straight ahead, fixated. I heard him mutter, "She's there. She *is*."

Aimee pressed herself back against the aft bulkhead, one hand clutching a storage box for balance, her expression flat and unreadable. I hoped my mien was the same for just a little longer. The sky grew darker, heavy, dangerous clouds gathering to the west, the wind hostile and biting. Dave never faltered. It wasn't half as bad as when we'd been chased off. They didn't want to scare us away this time. I glanced at Aimee. Black marble eyes bored into me, watching like a hawk. I nodded to myself.

Time. I swung off the bridge and went below to get my jacket.

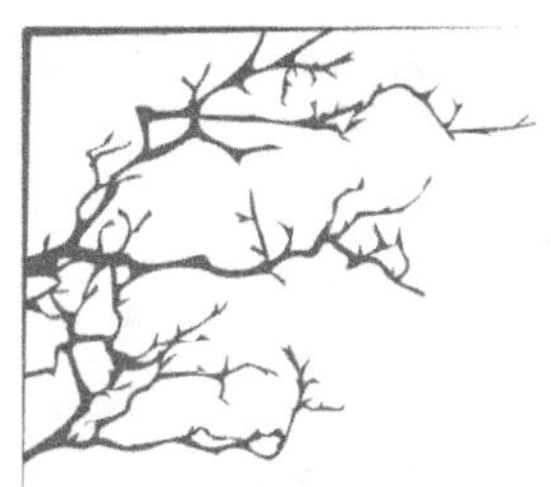

Chapter 17

We entered Duncan Bay, O'Connor on the foredeck at the anchor stay. Chain sang and steel splashed in choppy waters. Suddenly he cursed above the crying wind.

"Jaysus!" He gripped the railing, leaning far over, then started working his way rapidly aft, shouting desperately. "Shanna! Hang on, girl!"

A moment later he clambered over the port rail, screaming frantically. I was amidships with the dinghy. I yelled to him and sprinted forward, heard Dave screaming from the bridge. I ran as hard as I could and dived. My fingers closed on O'Connor's jacket and I heaved with all my might as he lunged outward.

"Let go!" he shrieked. "She's drowning!" He wrenched free, almost taking me with him. I thrust my arm through the railing, grasped only air. Freezing water hit me in the face as he plunged into the dark, churning bay. I glimpsed him once, striking hard, kicking deeper, reaching for something only he could see. Then he was gone. Dave pounded up, chest heaving.

"Christ Jesus!" Dave ripped his jacket off, began tearing at his boot laces. "Get a line! Get a fucking line!"

I hesitated. O'Connor was gone. Nothing could save him, I knew it in my heart, but I also knew Dave had to try. With a curse of my own I dashed to the nearest bulkhead, grabbed a ring buoy and line. Dave was on the rail in just his pants, balancing precariously as the *Lady* rose and fell on the heaving bay. Then he followed O'Connor in.

He tried. God knows he tried. I lost count of how many times he went down after his friend. More times than I could have, I know that, but in the end exhaustion won. He was barely able to grasp the ring as Aimee and I hauled him back aboard. He lay on the deck, sobbing for breath, tears mixed with cold water trickling down his cheeks.

"I will get a blanket," Aimee panted.

I nodded wordlessly and sat down next to Dave, forearms draped over my knees.

"Liam." Dave's clenched fist pounded weakly on the wet deck. "Liam..."

Aimee returned and wrapped a brown wool blanket around his quaking shoulders. He continued to hit the deck without any strength, oblivious to all but his grief. Aimee stood slowly, gazing down at him. Then she looked at me. "I am so sorry-"

Before she could finish I was on my feet, grabbing her bicep and dragging her with me. I slammed her against the superstructure by the empty buoy hook. "That's enough!" I spat. "Shut up before I throw you in after the poor bastard."

"You are hurting me," she whimpered, struggling weakly.

I only tightened my grip. "I thought we'd at least make it onto the beach before you tried to kill us." I jerked her up on her toes. "Who made him see that?" I shook her hard. "You? Did you make O'Connor see Shanna under the water?" She only sobbed in protest, blubbering about the Darkness as the wind whipped her midnight hair. What was Dave going to see? What was *I* going to see? I snarled under my breath. "Who's the Darkness, Aimee? Who is it really?"

She grimaced, tears flowing. "I do not know what you mean. The Darkness is the Darkness. Why are you doing this?" I drew back, breathing hard. Maybe she didn't know. "No..." Aimee whimpered. "I do not."

As soon as she uttered those words I knew. My free hand cocked to execute a *shuto* strike. I should have at least knocked her cold and part of me said to kill her, but at the last instant I checked. Her eyes, maybe. Huge, moist, and darkly ingenuous. Or maybe my own doubt. I never found Jo's bracelet. My arm fell to my side. I released her and stepped back. "Shit."

She said nothing, merely rubbed her upper arm and stared. Behind me, Dave climbed to his feet. Over his shoulder, from the thick pine forest, smoke rose. He turned, following my gaze. "God damn," he breathed. Then louder, "God damn it!" He threw off the blanket and in a flash was at the dinghy, barefoot and shirtless. Knowing it was suicide, I climbed in with him and helped Aimee in. There was no other choice, not really. Never had been.

Dave pulled hard on the oars, his muscles bunching against the roiling waters of Duncan Bay until we grounded on the deserted beach. I vaulted the gunwale into knee deep water. Ignoring the cold shock I grabbed my side and struggled forward. Dave did the same and together we dragged the little boat clear of the bay as Aimee crouched, clinging to a thwart. Bare-chested, no shoes, Dave took off at a dead run into the woods. Aimee scrambled out of the dinghy, shouting for him to wait. He didn't even look back. She turned to me. "Stop him. He will be lost."

No, he wouldn't. Dave would go right where they wanted him, like a moth to flame. I took Aimee by the arm and thrust her ahead of me. "Dave won't get lost, but I might. You can lead the way."

With an anxious look over her shoulder she set off along the narrow path. We were soon surrounded by moaning pines, the wind sliding malevolently through the boughs. Beyond the tops an already black sky darkened more with every step. I ignored both it and Aimee. Before long we came to the clearing where once music played and voices lifted. Tonight the bonfire was anything but cheerful. Sticks, branches, thick limbs, and even split logs rose, heaped in a conical pattern about a tall, rugged, rough-hewn pole in the center. The pole was a full two feet in diameter, eight or ten feet high, the timber pile around its base a head taller than a man. Lashed in the midst of this Sena strained at her bonds.

The pyre burned ferociously, flames well fed, an impenetrable barrier that leaped ever higher. Dave ran around the blazing circle searching madly for a way through to rescue the woman. Smaller branches snapped and popped beneath the ever increasing roar of the conflagration. When the first tongues of flame reached Sena she began to scream, worse than a nightmare, worse than the awful dream memory Mick had shown me. Smoke curled from Sena's black pants, from her shirt sleeves. Blonde hair smoldered, then crinkled as her clothing ignited. She wrenched hard trying to free herself and I heard a shoulder dislocate. Her cries rose to a piercing, soul-twisting shriek of terror and pain on tidal waves of heat heavy with the stench of seared flesh.

Dave bellowed and charged through shimmering, super-heated air. Knowing I couldn't stop him, I nevertheless tried. The terrific heat drove me back after only a few steps. I shielded my face as Dave crashed into the inferno in a volcanic cascade deluging me and driving me farther away. The fire roared louder, a frightful, living beast consuming all.

I staggered to where the air was bearable, my face and the backs of my hands red as Dave's final crazed scream of frenzy and despair echoed like the Devil's own laughter. I dropped to all fours, fighting for breath. Eventually I managed to lift my head and look around. The burning pyre cast long, evil shadows on darkened pines, the screams dying away to haunting echoes. The nauseating odor of charred human flesh lay as a sickening pall over the clearing, the foulest funereal draping polluting the memories of that place, burying them in smoke and vile night. And it nearly hid a slight, singular redolence I barely discerned. If I hadn't expected it, I might never have noticed. I climbed stiffly to my feet. Aimee stood a short distance behind me. Movement to my left caught my eye. I turned, feet shifting for balance, arms at my sides.

Twenty-five feet, no more, Mick was there as I knew she must be. Firelight again burnished her oval features, though it couldn't have been a more antithetical picture than the one I held so close to my heart. She was the same as when I first met her and when I last saw her – loose black pants and shirt, chestnut brown hair braided, eyes wide and searching – but tonight was nothing like that occasion and nothing since in between. Death surrounded me and it was her fault. She'd chosen me, tricked me, lied to me and finally led me here to die because she was a witch and the stories were all true. Every one of them. I let these thoughts fill my mind.

Off to Mick's left, wrapped in her grey cloak and shadows, Docent Edrea appeared, either from the woods or from thin air. It didn't matter, as long as she was there. She seemed untroubled by the loathsome smell. I gave her and her sensibilities no more consideration, my anger all for Mick. I thrust an accusing finger at the brunette and yelled hoarsely. "God damn you, witch! God damn you to hell!"

Her eyes went even wider in shock and she started forward. "Kim, no!"

I took a tottering step toward her, then another. "It wasn't enough you used me, you had to use Dave and O'Connor, too. You had to *kill* them. Why? For Christ's sake, *why Dave and Liam?*"

Her lips formed a denial, unheard above crackling flames and she held up a hand as if to stop me, warn me off. Her eyes beseeched me. I continued my advance undeterred. "O'Connor saw Shanna in the water. You made him see that and he's dead at the bottom of Duncan Bay." Another step. "You sent the dreams to Dave." Without turning or taking my eyes from her I stabbed viciously at the consuming holocaust. "You fucked him up so bad he walked right into the fire."

"That is not so..." She retreated a step, one hand covering her mouth.

I was close now, maybe ten feet from her. "I dreamed, too. You were running through the woods. Am I supposed to follow you and be killed there? Who's going to do it, Mick? You? Aimee? *Who?*" I risked one impatient glance, no more. Docent Edrea stood where she'd first appeared, a trace of a smile on her thin lips. It was all I needed to know. I gave my temper free rein and hammered Mick without mercy. "All this to kill Anton. And I'm the only one left that knows what you did. I'm the last one that knows what you are. The job's almost done, isn't it? *Come on.*" I tore open my jacket. "Put the fucking knife right in my heart instead of my back."

Mick stared, paralyzed. I reached into my jacket, into the pocket sewn inside. My fingers closed on the blade of one razor-sharp shuriken. Mick's features contorted with the beginning of horrified realization.

"You killed my friends," I said, voice cold. The throwing star emerged.

"Noo!" With a keening wail she dropped to her knees, fists to her temples, surrendering to her fate, though whether out of guilt or love I couldn't guess. I stopped, well within range, and cocked my arm for an overhand throw. Everything hinged on this moment.

"Run, Mick," I told her softly. "Run into the woods in case I miss. In case I'm wrong."

In that single frozen instant her eyes flickered with comprehension as I shifted my hips to attack in another direction. Edrea must have understood, too, in that last heartbeat as my arm came down and under, then snapped out, wrist flicking sharply in an underhand throw. Her eyes widened as well, the right one just in time to admit a blade of the throwing star. Passing through the Gateway to the Brain, the silent weapon struck her down. She collapsed without a sound, taking with her the Darkness from this place.

Straightening, I regarded my handiwork for a few seconds, the hot crackle of the bonfire the only sound in the forest. I walked slowly to the tree line where Edrea lay. It took a minute, but I found them there in the pine needles, three crushed butts where she'd waited. One still smoldered. I bent, nose wrinkling at the odor of cinnamon, and picked it up. I studied it for a moment, then looked at where the Darkness fell. Glittering flames reflected in the shuriken's four remaining polished lengths as blood from Edrea's ruptured eye socket welled black around the fifth. Thick rivulets worked their way down her cheek, past her lips, and slowly filled her open mouth. The other eye stared sightless at a gradually clearing sky through the still treetops where, one by one, the stars winked on. I looked at the cigarette butt once more. *Who among us is not susceptible.*

I turned my hand over, letting the butt fall to the ground, and walked away.

I SPENT THE NIGHT WITH Mick, in the cabin near the clearing. As before there were no lights, but I moved as if in a dream I'd had many times, my steps certain even in the dark of a new moon. I closed the windows on a mild evening and the smell from the smoldering remnants of the fire. When I lay in bed I could hear water lapping the shore from beyond the hushed forest. Mick lay beside me, close without touching. Neither of us undressed. For what seemed an eternity I stared at the ceiling, waiting for her to speak. To thank me, maybe. Or apologize. She could have explained, even. I don't know. I probably wouldn't have accepted any explanation other than one that conformed to my theory, but it seemed to me she ought to have something to say after all this. The woman uttered not a word.

I thought of Dave and O'Connor, wishing with all my heart that what happened hadn't, that I hadn't led them down a path that ended with me wishing and them gone. And I thought about Joanna, wishing just as hard, but with no more expectation of fulfillment. Wishes really aren't worth a pinch of batshit. I couldn't help wondering, too, if the cemetery dreams hadn't been cultivated for a reason, seeds planted years ago to grow with a horrible purpose. In a way I wished I'd never met Mick the Witch. And of course she knew I was thinking that. She sobbed quietly in the stillness.

"Is that true?" I whispered. "Did you kill Joanna? Did she have to die? Did all this have to happen?"

"How can I answer that?" she said thickly. "I wish it were not so. I wish much were not so, but there are things in my world you cannot imagine."

Wonderful things and terrible things, thrust good and bad upon one without choice. I stayed silent for a time, listening to the faint lapping sounds drifting up from Duncan Bay. Eventually I said, "They offered me immortality. I refused."

"I would expect no less from you."

I don't know if I should have said what I said next, but I said it. "They told me you could live. That you don't have to die at thirty. They offered that." I closed my eyes and whispered, "I turned them down, Mick."

"I know." She began to cry softly. For a time I lay with my hands on my chest, listening to her sob, then after a while I rolled over and took Mick in my arms. She clung to me, holding on until the dawn finally came.

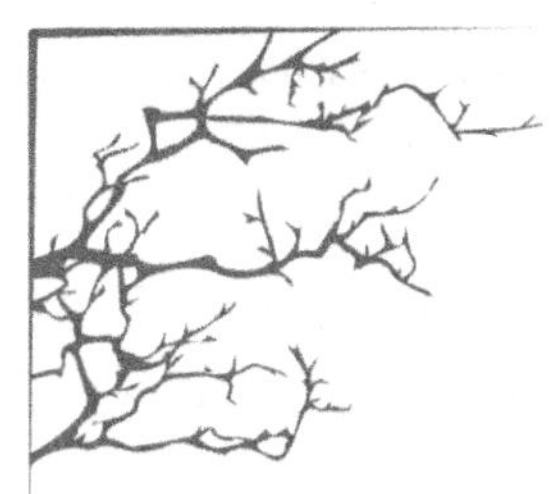

Chapter 18

A gentle breeze blew off the lake as Mick and I stood on the beach just beyond the trees. At the water's edge the emerald-eyed Shanna helped O'Connor coil the dinghy's bow line. Off to one side Dave talked quietly with Sena. I saw the statuesque blonde hand him a small, black cloth parcel. For a long minute I continued to watch the *Lady*'s captain and her mate. Then I turned to Mick and said simply, "I have to go."

"They will await you in the great city. Men without hearts."

"Probably."

"You could stay. Here."

I couldn't. I think she knew that. I wanted to believe that we'd met by chance in Jack's Place. I wanted to believe that all she wanted was a ride home and that that was all I'd done, but the whole experience argued otherwise. I saw O'Connor drown. I saw Dave and Sena burn to death. I glanced over my shoulder at the dinghy, glad that those things hadn't happened, but understandably reticent. I'd never know what thoughts, what dreams, were mine and which were someone else's. I'd never know what was real.

Mick stared at her feet, hands clasped before her, and whispered, "I love you."

I wanted to believe that, too. Maybe they could control us – maybe Mick could and maybe she wouldn't do that – but I'd never know for sure. I couldn't even be sure I loved her.

"Will you ever return?" she asked in a small, choked voice.

"I don't know. Will you ever go back to the M?"

"Before, I would have said never. After you are gone I cannot say what my answer might be."

It was my turn to inspect my sneakers. I nodded without comment. Mick's words offered a fragment of hope for us if I would accept it, but in truth there existed no reason for her or her sisters to return to the Sovereignty, any personal hope notwithstanding. And I had done all I could. The Darkness was dead. Isle Royale was safe for them now.

"Is it?"

Her words brought my head up sharply to find nothing but empty forest confronting me. Mick the Witch had vanished leaving only the fading echo of her question. I stood gazing deep into the pines until at last it was gone.

"Murayama! Shake a leg!" Dave's boarding call drifted up from the water's edge. Sena was nowhere to be seen, likewise Shanna. I waved okay and started walking. Half way there I turned for one last look. The forest remained, silent and mysterious, as concealing as the day I first set foot on the beach. The morning was pleasant enough, but now the island felt deserted. If they didn't want to be found...

I climbed into the dinghy, Dave in the stern, one hand on the till, while O'Connor readied oars. The *Shady Lady* rode sedately at anchor in the middle of the bay, but I kept watch on the trees as we drew off. Maybe Mick hadn't lied to me. Maybe. But someone had. As O'Connor pulled hard, leaving it all behind, I caught myself wondering if I'd really hit my mark with the shuriken.

And if I did, had it been the right one after all.

www.ingramcontent.com/pod-product-compliance
Lightning Source LLC
Chambersburg PA
CBHW071326140726
47996CB00005B/1847